CHADWICK'S EPIC REVENGE

CHADWICK'S EPIC REVENGE

Lisa Doan

Illustrated by
Natalie Andrewson

Roaring Brook Press
New York

*For all the downtrodden and tyrannized
who are diligently planning their next move.*

—L.D.

CHAPTER ONE

By the time I heard the news, the rumor mill was at a fever pitch. Principal Horatio Merriweather had mysteriously disappeared just days before the end of the school year. Marilee Marksley, a girl with her finger firmly on the social pulse of Wayne Elementary, prepared to hold a breaking news briefing on the bleachers.

The rumors connected the disappearance of Principal Merriweather to my nemesis, Terry Vance, aka the Nile crocodile. (It is technically true that I'm the only person who calls him the Nile crocodile. I've never been able to get a nickname for him off the ground, though I've made some valiant attempts, including: the piranha, the rattlesnake, the jackal, the viper, the assassin, and the deathstalker scorpion.)

The popular kids settled themselves around Marilee like planets around a sun. I, Chadwick Musselman, was slightly farther out in the orbit—not Mercury, so close that I was bathed in Marilee's light, but not Pluto in the darkness of the outer reaches of the bleacher galaxy either. Someday soon, I planned to rocket myself closer to the sun and sit next to Mars, otherwise known as the glorious Jana Sedgewick. (Mars is the red planet and Jana has red hair. Coincidence? I think not.)

Rory took the bleachers two at a time and threw himself down next to me. "Well," he whispered, "what did she say? What happened to Merriweather?"

"She hasn't said anything yet," I whispered back.

Marilee rose and slightly bowed her head. That was the signal. The bleachers became as silent as deep space.

"I saw the whole thing," Marilee said, solemnly raising her head and gazing across her bleacher galaxy. "I saw it with My Own Eyes."

I elbowed Rory and nodded. Marilee was the acknowledged Queen Bee of rumors and gossip because she saw everything with Her Own Eyes. It was almost like she brought extra eyes in her backpack each

morning and rolled them down every hallway in the school.

"Principal Merriweather pushed Terry Vance's face in a toilet bowl and flushed," she continued, acting out the movement of pushing down a handle.

"Wait," Jana of the glorious red hair said to Marilee.

"That must have happened in the boys' bathroom. Were you in there?"

"Not likely," Marilee said with a sniff. "Everyone knows that your average boys' bathroom is a terrarium of germs and diseases aggressively searching for host bodies."

I glanced around to see if any guy would challenge that description of the boys' bathroom. Nobody did and, to be fair, it sounded pretty accurate.

"What I saw," Marilee continued, "with My Own Eyes was Terry Vance walking out of the bathroom with his hair wet. Merriweather came out behind him, muttering, 'I did not flush!' Now Merriweather is gone. What could be more obvious, people? One plus one equals two."

"Did Terry do something horrible?" Jana asked. "I mean, why else would Principal Merriweather flush his face in a toilet?"

"Why is Jana wondering if Terry did something horrible?" I whispered to Rory. "Does she not understand the mind of the Nile crocodile at all? All the guy thinks about is doing horrible things. One false move and he'll hunt you down with relentless and horrible vengeance."

"Relentless and horrible vengeance sounds like a movie trailer," Rory said. "You act like you're a spy on the run from corrupt government officials. Which you're not, in case you were wondering."

I ignored Rory's attempt to minimize my situation. Terry Vance had been stalking me since the first grade over one extremely minor incident. So minor an incident that I have to believe that nobody was truly at fault. I suspect I exaggerate in even calling it an incident. Perhaps it was only a slight mishap. Unfortunately, that slight mishap had led to years of a deadly dance between the hunter and the hunted.

Mostly, I was the hunted. In fourth grade, I'd had a moment of wild-eyed optimism and decided I wasn't going to take it anymore. I would become a hunter myself. My first and last hunting expedition consisted of pulling out Terry's chair as he sat down. It worked—he fell on the floor—but my victory was surprisingly short-lived. He had looked up at me with an expression that made my heart temporarily stop beating. I could barely sleep that night, wondering if I would wake up and find him standing over me with a hatchet.

At our annual Scout camping trip a week later,

I'd even mentioned the hatchet scenario to our den leader. I was assured there were no dangerous weapons at the campsite. There was, though. Terry didn't take his revenge by chopping me to pieces and burying me in the forest. Instead, he filled my shampoo bottle with a ladies' hair removal product. Clumps of my hair fell out while we shouted our den yell on the bus ride home. (I was nicknamed Patches until it grew back.) After that, I did my best to keep away from the crocodile's habitat, counting on my gazelle-like swiftness to keep me alive. Sometimes I was fast enough, sometimes I wasn't.

Poor Principal Merriweather hadn't stood a chance against Terry Vance. Merriweather was too nervous to be a school principal. He never just walked down the halls—he edged down them, sliding along the lockers with his head darting in all directions like a bird watching for cats.

One time, he collapsed in the cafeteria when a new kid named Barry slapped him on the back and shouted, "What's up, Mr. M.?" (Rory and I helped him up and got him a carton of milk to soothe his shattered nerves.)

Every day after the last bell, Merriweather sprinted

to his Ford Fiesta and peeled out of the parking lot, hunched over the steering wheel, tires screeching. If I had been his guidance counselor, I would have recommended he change careers and become a monk sitting quietly by himself in a remote mountainside temple.

I could just imagine what had happened with Terry Vance. The Nile crocodile had floated patiently, his glassy eyes unblinking on the surface of the water, until poor Merriweather teetered on the riverbank of insanity. Then, in one explosive lunge, Merriweather was no more.

"I bet," I whispered to Rory, "that Vance got in trouble for something, then in retaliation he burned down the principal's house, or kidnapped his dog, or cut the brake lines on his Ford Fiesta. Merriweather went crazy and used the first weapon he could get his hands on, which just happened to be a toilet."

Rory snorted, which was his usual response to my theories. He was my best friend, but he lacked my fine-tuned imagination. Rory would only believe Terry Vance had cut the brake lines on Merriweather's Ford Fiesta if he saw Terry standing next to the car holding wire cutters and saying, "I just cut the brake lines on this Ford Fiesta."

"I don't know *why* Merriweather did it," Marilee said. "But I do know his likely whereabouts. I heard, with My Own Ears, my mom talking to Candy's mom on the phone. My mom said, 'Principal Merriweather was spotted at the airport?' Then she said, 'He ran through security?' Then she said, 'What does Terry Vance have to do with it?' Then she said, 'What does that mean—hiding in the backstreets of Bangkok?'

"So," Marilee said, "we now know that either Merriweather got arrested for running through security at the airport or he's hiding in the backstreets of Bangkok, Thailand. One thing is certain: our principal flushed Terry Vance's face in a toilet and fled the scene. We will never see him again."

Marilee bowed her head. The briefing was over.

I hoped Merriweather had made it to Bangkok. Once he got settled, he could go find that remote mountainside temple where the perpetually hunted take a rest. I thought I might go there myself one of these days.

Fifth grade had come to a close with a missing

principal and a Nile crocodile still cruising the waters of Wayne Elementary.

* * *

"The school board had better do something about Flush Gate," my mom said, handing around the peas nobody was going to eat. Me, my dad, and my brother waited patiently for her to pass around the corn on the cob. The peas were just my mom's opening gambit—she liked to see if she could catch one of us so ravenous that we might break down and eat something disgusting. Mark sometimes cracked; he was a hulking football player and would pour all kinds of junk down his throat in pursuit of more muscles—powders, liquefied salads, protein bars that tasted like sawdust and egg yolks, to name a few.

"Nobody wants peas?" she asked, getting the bowl back untouched.

Mark and I mumbled something about maybe wanting peas later. My dad said, a little too loudly, "Hate peas."

My mom slowly set the bowl down and stared at him. My dad, seeing he was about to drown in a hurricane of nutritional facts about peas, lobbed a classic diversion in her direction. The old "agree heartily" maneuver.

"I agree heartily with you about Flush Gate," he said, grabbing two ears of corn. "The school board had better do something."

"Really," my mom said, watching my dad ruin a whole stick of butter by rolling an ear of corn across the top. "What do you think they should do?"

Mark and I looked with interest at my dad. I was pretty sure he had not spent one second thinking about what the school board should do. I was not even sure if he knew what Flush Gate was.

My dad stared down at the melting stick of butter, planning his next move like he was a Russian chess master. Then he cleared his throat and said, "The more important question is, what do *you* think the school board should do?"

Well played, Dad.

Though my mom was perfectly aware that my dad had just dodged her question, she usually agreed with his opinion that her own thoughts probably were more important than his.

"For one," she said, "I find that letter they sent to all the parents ridiculous. They claim there was no face flushing, but they have no explanation as to why Principal Merriweather disappeared. Or where he disappeared to. And they say nothing about the eyewitness. Marilala whatever. She saw it with her own eyes."

"Marilee," I corrected her. "Marilee Marksley."

"Number two," my mom continued, "the next principal must be firmly anti-flushing. We cannot tolerate a school principal who flushes kids' faces in the toilet. What if Chadwick says or does something annoying? Are we to expect his face will be flushed? Don't you think he would be traumatized by something like that?"

My dad, having been asked questions that aren't really questions before, did not comment on whether or not I would be traumatized.

"Merriweather only flushed one face," I said, "and it happened to be Terry Vance's face so it was totally justified. Also, I'm not annoying."

My mom smiled at me. "Of course you're not, honey. Not to us."

And so, the summer began with the questions

that would consume our dinner table conversation until the fall—what had really happened in the boys' bathroom, what was the school board going to do about it, and where was Merriweather?

* * *

"Where are we going?" Rory asked.

"To our destiny," I said, showing our badges to old Mr. Clarkson at the community-pool gate.

Mr. Clarkson stared down at our badges and then held them up to the light, as if we were con men trying to scam our way into the pool with forged documents. This, I knew, would happen every day of the summer. He had no memory at all, and every time he saw us would be like the very first time.

"Destiny?" Rory said. "That sounds like we're going to die."

Mr. Clarkson, having satisfied himself that we were properly credentialed, opened the gate.

"We won't die," I said. "Just follow my lead."

It was our first day at the community pool, and I

had planned out where we would put our towels. The first day would dictate how the whole summer would go. Last year, I had not been pool savvy and we had ended up with spots next to the diving board. We got cannonballed for three months straight, and it had not gone unnoticed by the clique of popular kids that hung out at the pool. I believe, toward the end, they were even paying other people to cannonball us.

This year, I had an ambitious plan. I would not get cannonballed. Instead, I would deploy a method I had invented called "lurking and creeping" to drastically improve my social standing. Becoming one of the in crowd, or at least one of the nearby the in crowd, would lead to Jana Sedgewick of the glorious red hair noticing me. Noticing, I was sure, was the first step to liking. After noticing, the sky was the limit.

Campaign Lurk and Creep had commenced.

CHAPTER TWO

I dragged Rory through the pool gates and hooked my thumb in the direction of the Snack Shack. I had chosen that area of the deck for a couple of reasons. One, it was far away from the diving board and cannonballs. Two, Marilee Marksley had already established an office right next to the snack stand. She had brought her own lounge chair and she had a folding table next to it stacked with papers and sticky notes. I was sure that spot would be her official news headquarters for the rest of the summer. Being as near as possible to Marilee's chair was crucial to Campaign Lurk and Creep.

I had pretty much memorized all the cliques at school—big, small, and overlaps. Jana was in a small clique with her best friends, Bethany Belkin and Carmen Rodriguez. But that small clique was part of Marilee's bigger clique—an overlap. Me and Rory were our own small clique. So far, we didn't have an overlap. That's what I planned to change. Rory and I would slowly and invisibly drift into Marilee's bigger clique, thereby becoming members of the same overlap clique as Jana.

It was vital that I execute the maneuver over the summer, at the pool. The one place I knew I was safe from Terry Vance was the pool. You'd think a Nile crocodile would be hanging out in the water nonstop, but I had never seen him there. While I was free of that menace, I would casually lurk into Jana's overlap. Overlaps, I had figured out, were the key to everything.

Around the middle of last year, the whole fifth grade had suddenly been consumed with talking about who liked who. A rumor would go around about a couple and they would be sitting next to each other at lunch and everybody would be looking at them. As far as I could tell, being in a couple didn't involve much more than that. What I noticed, though, was that their coolness seemed to exceed the sum of their parts. It was like there was some kind of synergy in sitting next to a girl. I knew I could definitely use that kind of a boost and was determined to become one half of a power couple. That's when I looked around and noticed Jana and her fiery hair. (I would have pegged myself as a guy with a blond on his arm, so who knew?)

Just one small problem. On the savannah of elementary school, Jana was at the head of the herd and I was shuffling along in the middle. Almost immediately after deciding that I liked Jana, I noticed that there weren't any "who likes who" crossovers. All the liking was concentrated on who was nearby, in their own clique or overlaps. The answer was obvious enough—get nearby, get into an overlap.

Rory followed me as we made our way to our new spot. I walked past Marilee and casually said, "Hey."

She lowered her sunglasses to look at me, then put them back on and went back to gnawing on a frozen Snickers bar.

It could not have gone more perfectly. Her sunglasses move wasn't a "come on into my overlap clique" signal, but it wasn't a "get out of my territory" signal either. It was neutral. Step one was a success.

I picked a spot about ten feet from Marilee, not wanting it to be obvious that I was trying to creep into her group, and laid my towel down.

"Oh, I get it," Rory said, throwing his towel on the ground. "It'll be faster to get snacks from here. And we won't get wet from cannonballs. Good thinking. My mom made me swear I wouldn't eat any junk food at the pool, but I had my fingers crossed underneath the table. She doesn't know that my dad already gave me money and said, 'Ice cream until you drop—that's what summer is all about.' Between your snack drawer and the Snack Shack, it's going to be a magically sweet and salty vacation."

I didn't bother to mention that my mom has started to comment on how fast things have been disappearing out of our snack drawer. I had already hinted to her that I might have seen Mark eating three Ring Dings at a time, to throw the suspicion off Rory. I didn't know how many calories Rory took in on a daily basis, I only knew that most of the calories were coming from my house due to Mrs. Richardson's strict ideas about nutrition.

The year before, Rory's mom had decided to dramatically change her lifestyle, which had dramatically changed Rory's lifestyle. Where once they had lived on all kinds of glorious fried food, rich pastries, and a sugar bowl on the table ready to pour its sweet goodness over any kind of cereal, now they lived on kale smoothies and salads. Rory's kitchen cabinets were filled with bags of seeds and nuts, like a family of birds lived there. Nobody really understood how Rory's mom thought it was possible to sustain life on what she brought home from the farmers' market, but she was pretty obsessed with the idea. Rory and his dad spent half their lives plotting how to get sugar and salt.

"I think I'll just go have a look at the inventory," Rory said, gazing lovingly at the Snack Shack.

"Don't go yet," I said. The next part of my plan to creep into Marilee's overlap was to do a typical guy move in front of her. I had watched her guy friends last year and they were always throwing themselves into the water and roughhousing. She seemed to appreciate their efforts.

I shoved Rory and said, "Beat you into the water!"

"No you won't," Rory said, pushing past me and

jumping in the pool. I was right behind him, determined to make a decent splash.

I belly flopped into the water and felt as if I had been hit with a stun gun. I should have realized why nobody else was swimming—it was one degree short of an ice cube.

Rory clawed his way to the surface and let out a little scream. I bit down on my tongue to stop myself. Marilee was looking right at us.

Rory dog-paddled to the side, heaved himself out, and lay on the cement, panting and soaking up the heat from the pavement. I desperately wanted to get out, but I didn't want it to look like I hadn't meant to jump into the Arctic Sea. Not while Marilee was watching.

I pretended I couldn't care less that it was cold and started swimming around in circles with a frozen smile on my face.

I noticed I was starting to draw attention. I supposed Rory and I were the only ones who had not known the pool was thirty-three degrees. Just when I decided I had done enough to convince all these onlookers that I could handle it, Jana cruised in with Bethany and Carmen trailing behind her.

She looked at me and then pointed me out to her friends.

Jana Sedgewick was noticing me. I felt like I better do something interesting. I did a handstand at the shallow end, then I pushed off and swam underwater all the way to the deep end to show how long I could hold my breath. I did a lap of backstroke.

I had thought I would warm up as I got used to

the temperature, but instead I was starting to feel paralyzed and was possibly drowning.

As I began to sink, I used the last of my strength to flail to the side of the pool. I casually whispered to Rory, "I can't feel my arms."

Rory dragged me out, with a lot of complaining about how I was dead weight, but my arms weren't all that powerful even when they were working properly.

I struggled to my feet and noticed that my legs had turned a sickly white, as if all the blood had raced somewhere deeper in my body in revolt from the frigid pool water. They wobbled underneath me like all the bones had been surgically removed.

I attempted a look of stoicism and glanced around me. I couldn't tell if Jana had realized I was about to drown. Or whether Marilee had seen it. Jana and her friends surrounded Marilee, just like they always did on the bleachers. I supposed I'd find out eventually if Marilee had seen what happened—it would make its way into her news briefing. "I saw, with My Own Eyes, Musselman drown in the pool because he didn't check the temperature."

"I'm not going back in there until July," Rory said.

I staggered to my towel while Rory followed me saying, "Why did you stay in there so long? You can hardly walk. Didn't you notice it was cold?"

Just then, Marilee rose majestically from her lounge chair and her friends all sat down around her. I collapsed onto my sun-warmed towel and pointed at her so Rory would stop asking me why I had stayed in the pool.

"Ground rules for the summer, people," Marilee said. "If you want to hang out and hear what I have seen with My Own Eyes, that's cool, as long as you bring me snacks. My personal friends—you know who you are—don't have to bring me snacks, but my on-lookers do."

Marilee paused. I grabbed my wallet. Rory and I were definitely still onlookers. One towel placement did not make somebody part of an overlap. It would take more time and effort than that. Campaign Lurk and Creep involved days and days of casually creep-ing closer. Eventually, we'd slip over the border of the overlap, but it would be so slow that it would seem like we'd always been there.

"What are you doing?" Rory asked.

I had struggled to my feet. "We're the onlookers," I whispered.

I walked as quickly as I could to the Snack Shack, using all my strength to hide the fact that my legs had turned into rubber. I bought a frozen Snickers. I had seen Marilee with a Snickers already, so it was a safe bet. There was too much at stake to make a gamble on a Three Musketeers or Reese's Peanut Butter Cups only to find out she hated them or was allergic.

I staggered to her chair and held out the frozen candy bar like it was an offering to an Aztec altar.

Marilee nodded graciously and took the candy bar. "Thank you, Chadwick," she said.

I attempted a dignified walk back to my towel, thrilled that Marilee Marksley knew my name. "She knows my name," I whispered to Rory as my legs gave way underneath me and I crashed down on my towel.

"She's Marilee," Rory whispered back, "she knows everybody's name. Why would you give her a candy bar when you've seen my food situation at home?"

"Now," Marilee said, "I shall reveal *two* breaking news stories. First up, just twenty-four hours ago, Mitchell Grand's mom gave him a military haircut. Mrs. Grand, I heard with My Own Ears, said it would be cooler in the summer. As you may recall, the sun was out all day yesterday. There was a basketball tournament at the YMCA. Outdoors. Can you put it all together, people? Mitchell Grand's whole head is severely sunburned and is now peeling off in sheets. In. Literal. Sheets. He was just spotted in the Walmart parking lot pulling off whole strips and throwing them on the ground. Birds are eating them as we speak. Mrs. Grand remains inside the store, talking to the pharmacist about what to do about it."

"Ew," Jana said. "I thought I might like him, but not if he's bald and pulling slabs of skin off his head to feed the birds. That's just gross."

"Ew indeed, Jana," Marilee said. "Ew indeed."

Jana was already considering who she liked? I silently thanked Mitchell Grand's mom for her incompetence.

"Now, on to the next story," Marilee continued. "Terry Vance, the student who was involved in the face-flushing incident that led to the disappearance of our principal, has flunked the fifth grade. I saw it with My Own Eyes."

"How did she *see* Terry flunking?" Rory whispered.

I didn't answer. Marilee's words were almost too much to take in.

"Terry claims," Marilee continued, "that Principal

Merriweather changed all his grades to Fs before fleeing to Thailand. Why is this newsworthy? Only because Terry Vance will become the tallest fifth grader in the history of Wayne Elementary and we will be there to witness it."

Terry Vance had flunked. He would stay in fifth grade. Not go to sixth grade. It was going to be the best summer ever. I was leaving the Nile crocodile behind—the tyranny of pranks was finally finished.

Marilee bowed her head and unwrapped the Snickers I had given her. The briefing was over. It had been the greatest briefing of my life.

I would be a sixth grader and Terry would still be a fifth grader. The sixth graders ruled the school. We had our own lounge, exclusively for sixth graders. We had special field trips. We had T-shirt day, when all the sixth graders wore wacky shirts. We even got a row of cafeteria tables right next to the windows. (I doubt that one was a school rule, it was just known.)

I would have one magical year of being on top before moving up to junior high and starting over at the bottom. I would be on top without Vance. The apex predator had just been demoted. As a lowly fifth grader, he was clawless and toothless. I would no longer be a flamingo wading along the banks of Wayne Elementary, wondering when my spindly legs would be snapped by his powerful jaws. I would leap over the crocodile's river and make my way to the safety of the sixth-grade savannah. Now I could focus all of my energy and concentration on creeping closer to Jana, without having to look over my shoulder for Terry Vance.

With any luck, Vance would keep flunking and never catch up to me. I felt like my chances were pretty decent. I could easily imagine how he would settle into the fifth grade, each year growing bigger and finding the easy prey too delicious to leave behind. There would come a time when Terry would be the only fifth grader to drive himself to school, probably in Principal Merriweather's stolen Ford Fiesta, running stop signs and swerving onto sidewalks all the way.

"Do you see what this means?" I asked Rory.

"Yup," Rory said. "Mitchell Grand will have to wear a hat for the whole summer. Supposedly, once you get one bad sunburn you have to be really careful and slather on the sunscreen."

"No," I said. "Vance. The Nile crocodile. He won't

be able to torture me anymore. I'll be in a higher grade. Not even Vance would dare breach the time-honored tradition about who is in charge. We'll be in charge. He'll just be a fifth grader. We'll be upstairs and he'll be downstairs."

Rory considered this. "That's good, Chadwick. Now you can finally let it go. This whole obsession with Terry was starting to take over your life. And take over my life."

"It's over now," I said, high-fiving Rory. "It's finally over."

* * *

Finding out I was free of Terry Vance began to change my whole personality. It started small, like I noticed that I had developed a swagger when I walked around at the pool. It was the kind of swagger I had noticed on popular guys that said, "That's right, I'm here, any questions?"

Each day, I inched our towels closer to Marilee and Jana. So far, Jana had not said anything about it.

That meant that if she had noticed, then she was for it. If she hadn't noticed, then it wasn't bothering her. Either way, it was all good.

When I went shopping with my mom for new swim trunks, I picked out a plaid print. Every other summer, I had only gotten as daring as a navy blue solid, but now I felt like I could pull off plaid. The trunks had a casual Ralph Lauren vibe and you couldn't tell that we bought them at Kmart.

I even started to feel like I had more muscles in my arms. Maybe it was the tan, I don't know, but there was a definite improvement. I had been so used to being the scrawny kid next to my King Kong brother that it was surprising to see this new me in the mirror. I was never going to have muscles ripping the seams of my shirts like Mark did, but my arms didn't look like toothpicks either.

Once, instead of handing Marilee her frozen Snickers, I shouted, "Heads up, Marksley," and threw it to her. She caught it and laughed and I stood there thinking, *Who are you, dude?* That inspired me to really go for it the next day. I bought two candy bars and threw them at Marilee *and* Jana. Marilee caught hers, but my candy offering took Jana by surprise. So yes, technically, I hit her in the face, but she ended up eating it. I took that to mean: message thrown and message received. The next move in Campaign Lurk and Creep was to actually say something to Jana.

I thought long and hard about what I would say. I could compliment her hair and compare it to a forest fire or Mars the red planet, but then she'd probably heard those a million times already. I could point out something original, like how one of her earlobes was slightly longer than the other one. But then I began to question whether it would be weird to be an earlobe noticer. I could accidentally run into her and we could laugh as we hit the pavement, but then you could never be sure how somebody would feel about getting knocked to the ground. In the end, I decided that saying something to her right off the bat was not going to be my style. Lurking and creeping closer to her overlap clique was working. At heart, I was a natural-born lurker.

I laid out my plan to my brother, Mark.

"What do you mean, creeping and lurking?" he asked.

"I will just be there, nearby. I've been doing it all summer at the pool. I'm slowly joining her overlap group without anybody really noticing. If I lurk around her enough, liking me will creep up on her all slow-like. Heck, for all I know it's already happening."

"So," Mark said, "you plan on just always being nearby. Silently nearby."

"And creeping closer," I said.

"How is she supposed to know you are liking her and not stalking her?"

"Because I don't look like a stalker," I said. "I look like a liker."

Mark folded his arms and stared at me. "Chadwick, girls aren't robots and they won't suddenly start liking you just because you're nearby. Take my advice on this one."

"First," I said, "I didn't say she would suddenly like me, I said it would creep up on her. Second, I threw a candy bar at her and she ate it. Third, your advice isn't always so perfect." I pointed to the scar on my left knee from some recent bad advice from Mark involving my newfound confidence, my bicycle, and a home-built ramp. "Apparently, you don't know as much about the physics of flight as you thought you did."

"I don't know anything about the physics of

flight," Mark said. "That's why I had you go first. But I do know something about girls. Cheryl and I have been dating for seven whole months. And I repeat, do not go with the lurking strategy. It will never work."

I decided to ignore Mark's advice. For one thing, Cheryl is the only sort-of-a-girlfriend he's had in his whole life. She shrugs more than speaks, and I'm not sure she actually knows she's dating him—she might just think he's a taxi service. For another, lurking and creeping were playing to my strengths—I was practically at the border of the overlap.

CHAPTER THREE

"Straight to the auditorium," Ms. Carson yelled over the waves of kids pouring out of buses.

It was the first day of school and we were heading into an assembly. There were no assigned seats in the auditorium so that meant it was go time on casually lurking around Jana Sedgewick at school. By the last day at the pool I had made it just inside the overlap. Now I had to transfer all that success to a different location.

School lurking would be a whole new ball game. The pool was a contained environment, but school was a moving target. I would have to be constantly alert to figure out where she would be and how I could casually be there, too.

Passing through the front doors, I noticed the school smelled just like always—a mix of chalk, magic markers, and bologna sandwiches. It felt different, though. As a sixth grader, I was king. The younger kids cautiously made their way inside. Those kids looked at me and Rory like we were highly important, and who was I to say they were wrong? I put on my pool swagger and swaggered down the hall.

Despite our kingly sixth-grade status, Rory and I were carried along by the crowd of students funneling into the hallway that led to the auditorium. It felt like we were a school of fish being driven into a net.

"My dad says it's confirmed—Merriweather is gone for good. He doesn't know if they found a new principal yet," Rory said.

"The school board had the whole summer to find one," I said over my shoulder. "They probably hired a Navy SEAL."

"Why?" Rory said.

"Because our last principal went insane. They need a 'take no prisoners' kind of guy. A SEAL will slam the crocodile's hand in a locker if he acts up."

"We don't know what Terry did to Principal Merriweather," Rory said, "or if he even did anything. Marilee's report was pretty flimsy, even for Marilee."

"We don't know the exact details of what he did," I said. "But whatever it was, it was a glimpse into the Nile crocodile's black soul that drove our principal to madness and forced him to move to Southeast Asia."

"We don't know that."

"Yes, we do. I am only glad that, thanks to his poor study habits, Terry is not my problem anymore. We are sixth graders and really don't have time to care about what he will be doing in the fifth grade for the second year in a row. He remains downstairs middle management, while we are the new upstairs chief executive officers. Didn't you notice how I totally ignored him on the bus? Like he was invisible?"

"You always ignore him on the bus," Rory said.

"I used to ignore him so that he wouldn't notice me," I said. "Today, I ignored him like he was invisible. Didn't you see the difference?"

"Not really," Rory said. "I was too busy trying to convince Jennifer Johnson to trade her peanut butter sandwich for my lettuce wrap. But then she found out the filling was lettuce too and she said no. What say *you* to a trade, my good man?"

"No," I said. If Mrs. Richardson made it, it was not just full of vegetables—there was probably even seaweed and a sprinkling of flaxseeds in there.

I burst through the auditorium doors and stood on my toes, searching for Jana. The place was packed, but Jana's red hair sticks out like a bonfire. (Another amazing benefit of a girl with red hair: you're never going to lose her in a crowd.)

She was down in the first row, sitting between Carmen and Bethany. I shoved and squeezed my way through the crowd, leaving Rory behind. I got a seat behind Jana. It wasn't right next to her, but it was my first attempt at lurking at school so I will call that a victory. And really, it was way closer than I ever got at the pool.

I casually leaned forward and smelled her hair. It reminded me of grass, sort of like a mowed lawn. Jana whispered to Carmen, "Can you believe it? I just looked at him and said, 'Whatever.'"

Carmen nodded. "I knew he was crushin' on you."

I sat back. Who were they talking about? It wasn't

me—Carmen Rodriguez didn't know my name. She just knew me as the lurking candy thrower.

Who else was trying to lurk near Jana? Hopefully, it was somebody like Clarke Crandall—an individual who owned a T-shirt that said, "Mathematicians make better pi." Every time he wore it he walked down the halls saying, "Get it? Pi like 3.14159 and pie like apple?" I could look like an excellent choice next to Clarke.

"Everybody! Quiet down!"

Ms. Grimeldi, the school's assistant principal, stood at the microphone. There was no sign of Merriweather so I supposed he really was gone for good.

The crowd shushed as stragglers jumped into their seats.

"Welcome to a brand-new school year," she said. "I am so happy to see each and every one of you." Ms. Grimeldi paused and stared at Terry Vance. He stared back.

"My first announcement today is that the school board has named me the new principal of Wayne Elementary."

Ms. Grimeldi was our new principal? That was hard to imagine. I had gotten used to her just following Merriweather around saying, "Sir, if you would only take a long and slow breath."

"Of course," Ms. Grimeldi continued, "I am honored and thrilled and I can promise you it will be an exciting year, filled with learning."

I tuned out the rest of her speech. Ms. Grimeldi was too far away from her own school years to remember anything about it. Filled with learning it was not. These were tense times on the savannah. Survival was the name of the game—learning was a distant second.

"And finally," Ms. Grimeldi said, "you will find a new class called group on your schedules. The school board felt that after last year's unfortunate departure of Principal Merriweather, we should work on improving communication. Group will be a safe place where you can talk about your feelings."

Half the auditorium erupted in moaning and yelps, and one guy in the back sounded like he had been shot. It was madness; there was no place on the savannah for feelings.

Bethany leaned over and whispered to Jana, "It will be like sharing secrets at a sleepover, except in school!"

I sat back. I had not known that was what occurred at girls' sleepovers. Rory and I drank a lot of soda and played video games when he slept at my house. What kind of secrets were they sharing? Would group be able to pry any secrets out of my own brain? I hoped not; there was a reason a person did not go around telling people that he had wet the bed until he was five years old and had only stopped when he was told he couldn't go to kindergarten. (Mrs. Musselman had worried that it was some kind of medical problem, but I had just not felt like getting up in the middle of the night.)

* * *

Group exceeded my worst expectations. As soon as I realized it would be a whole class about secret feelings, I had my fingers crossed to be in a group with Glenna Bradley and Marilee Marksley. Glenna had a lot of strong feelings about how she looked, and no matter how many times you said "No, they don't" or "I never noticed that," she said you were wrong and gave you more evidence to prove that her problem was real. She could have talked about the size of her arms until June. If she and Marilee were in my group, Marilee could have stepped in to fill any remaining minutes with an analysis of the size of everybody else's arms, based on what she had seen with Her Own Eyes. It would have been an impenetrable girl wall of talking, providing cover for those of us who had nothing to say. Little did I know, while I was mulling over the chances of getting through the whole year without saying anything, there was a bigger problem heading my way.

As I walked down the hall toward Mr. Samson's classroom, I saw Terry Vance coming the other direction. I thought he had a lot of nerve, he wasn't even supposed to be on our floor. The second floor was for sixth-grade classes only.

"Hey, Vance," I said, full of kingly coolness, "the fifth graders are downstairs."

"What of it?" Terry said, sneering at me.

What did he mean, what of it?

"You're supposed to be downstairs," I said. "You're not even allowed to be up here looking around."

"You're a piece of work, Mussel-*man*," Terry said, veering into Mr. Samson's classroom.

"Wait," I called after him. "You can't go in there!" I hurried after him to see what he was up to. It was crucial that I make him go back downstairs. Fifth graders had to be downstairs, he couldn't just come up here whenever he felt like it.

Terry had settled himself into a chair.

"This is not your class," I cried. "You flunked!"

"Yes, it is my class, and no, I didn't flunk," Terry said, looking amused. "I started that rumor just to get your hopes up. Worked pretty good, too."

"You didn't make it up," I said. "Marilee saw it with Her Own Eyes. She reported it at the pool over the summer."

"I might have mentioned something to her," the crocodile said, smiling.

I stared at Terry. This could not be true.

"I think I even told her that Merriweather changed all my grades to Fs before fleeing to Thailand," Terry said.

The reality of what he'd said was slowly sinking into my brain. He told Marilee he flunked, knowing the news would fly around like wildfire and I was sure to hear about it. All to get my hopes up. My hopes had been more than up, they had been in the stratosphere.

And now here he was. In sixth grade. In my group.

I fell into a chair and tried to revive my confidence. Terry Vance, purveyor of tacks and hair-removal shampoo, had just played a mind game on me. As I contemplated what that might mean for my future, the rest of my group filed in. They were exactly the people I didn't want to have in a group full of secret feelings. Where was Glenna Bradley when you actually needed her?

Rory. As best friends, we kept a respectful distance from each other's emotions. I had no idea what was torturing Rory's mind and hoped I never found out.

Jana. I wanted Jana to be my girlfriend. I doubted she would want to get involved with some guy who had a lot of feelings he wanted to talk about.

Bethany. Bethany was a walking and talking extension of Jana and thought whatever Jana thought, so really, Jana was in my group twice.

Suvi Singh. A girl I have tried to avoid since she moved here from India in the second grade. Suvi made me feel dumb. Unlike Rory, who made me feel like a Jeopardy! champion.

And worst of all, the Nile crocodile. Terry had not flunked. Not only had I not left him behind, but now I would be forced to view the inside of his diseased mind. I was pretty sure it was filled with knife fights, plans for a bank heist, and all the humiliating pranks he would pull on me this year. My swagger began to trickle out of my body like water going down a drain.

Mr. Samson, the science teacher, was our group leader. He made us put our chairs in a circle.

"Okay, settle down," Mr. Samson said. "The school board wants everybody to talk about their feelings. So here we go, who has any?"

Silence hung in the room like a fog. I had turned my chair so I wouldn't have to see Terry staring at me. He always stared at me a lot, but especially right after one of his pranks. I knew he'd be watching to see if the realization that he hadn't flunked had caused maximum damage. I was determined to ignore him. I had my own plans to worry about. Though I hadn't yet attempted to speak to Jana, I had waved at her a couple of times at the pool.

I stared at her until I caught her eye and casually waved.

She turned and looked behind her like I was waving to somebody else.

She didn't realize I was the candy guy from the pool! How was that possible? Maybe she would only recognize me if I were wearing the plaid shorts? I couldn't have done all that creeping and lurking for nothing.

"C'mon," Mr. Samson said, "somebody has to say something."

Rory raised his hand. I turned to him in horrified fascination like he had just offered himself up for sacrifice.

"Fine, Rory, go ahead," Mr. Samson said, rocking back in his chair.

"So," Rory said, "just a couple of years ago you could say, 'Hey, I want to be on the soccer team,' and then you were on it. And you got to play no matter what. But now you have to show how good you are. I'm against that."

"Everybody who goes to the tryout makes the team, if that's what you're worried about," Mr. Samson said.

"But you have to go to the tryout now."

"What are you afraid will happen at a tryout?" Mr. Samson asked, crossing his arms behind his head.

"I'll never know," Rory said. "I'm against trying out."

I elbowed Rory. I had already told him a million times that the world didn't care what he was against. He had a whole notebook, titled *Things I'm Against*, that he had been adding to since the third grade.

Suvi said, "How will you succeed in life if you're not willing to follow the rules?"

"I'll follow the rules after they get changed," Rory said.

"Foreigner," Suvi muttered.

Suvi called everybody except Ajay Gupta a foreigner, like we had all moved to Mumbai instead of her moving to the Philadelphia suburbs. Nobody ever said anything to her about it; getting into a debate with Suvi Singh was like arguing with a stadium full of Albert Einsteins. As far as I could tell, she had started memorizing Wikipedia the moment she had landed on our shores.

"Right," Mr. Samson said. "Thank you for expressing your concern about team tryouts, Rory. And thank you for your comments also, Suvi. Though

44

maybe you could refrain from calling everybody a foreigner."

Suvi folded her arms, so I guessed that was a no.

"Mr. Samson," Jana said, "that guy is talking about sports tryouts because he doesn't know how to talk about feelings. He might not even have them—I can't really tell. Some boys have them and some don't, but all girls feel feelings really deeply. Like, when the Bombtastics broke up last year, I was highly devastated. I even had to take their poster off my wall because I couldn't stand looking at it—we had been so happy! I'm only just starting to recover."

"It's true," Bethany said. "She was a total mess."

I made a mental note to find out about the Bombtastics. At some point in my Jana lurking, I would be forced to speak. Probably sooner than I had planned since she appeared to have no memory of me from the summer and had just referred to Rory as "that guy." The Bombtastics could be a great way to start a conversation. Mark pretends to like a show about a bunch of rich people living in England because one of the few sentences Cheryl has ever uttered to him was "I love *Downton Abbey*." I don't always trust Mark's advice, but I saw him work *Downton Abbey* into a random conversation once and Cheryl's eyelids flickered. For Cheryl, that's the height of enthusiasm, so I'm pretty sure he's onto something.

"Advising you about boy band breakups is way over my pay grade," Mr. Samson said, "and I'm pretty sure your theory on boys' feelings wouldn't hold up under scientific scrutiny." He rifled through the papers in his hand. "Wait a minute, here we go. There's a list of prompt questions to guide the discussion. Number one, how do you feel about your home life? Let's hear from someone who hasn't had a chance yet."

I pressed my body against my chair, hoping the plastic molecules and the molecules of my body would meld together and my chair would appear empty. As further insurance, I sent Mr. Samson mind-control messages—"I'm invisible! Look right through me! You do not see a person named Chadwick in this room!"

"Terry," Mr. Samson said, "how are things at home for you?"

"Fine," he said.

Typical. That's what I had planned to say if the molecule meld didn't work and I was still visible.

"Not true," Suvi said to Terry. "What about what you told me when I went to your house?"

"I didn't tell you anything," Terry said.

"Mr. Samson," Suvi said, "when I was in the fourth grade, my mother made me join the Girl Scouts. She said it would be an excellent way for me to further understand Americans. Among other dangerous activities, like learning how to build a fire, I was forced to sell cookies to strangers. Remember that, Terry?" she said.

"Not really," Terry said.

"I went to Terry's house," Suvi said, "and he grabbed a box of Thin Mints out of my hands and said his dad would pay me later. Then, just before he slammed the door in my face, he said, 'Too bad later actually means never.' Despite numerous attempts to collect the debt, I still have not been paid."

Terry snorted.

Finally, somebody else had viewed the real Terry Vance. I looked at him with my eyebrows raised, feeling oddly vindicated by Suvi's story.

"Any household with a median income would find the purchase of cookies well within reach. So you see, Mr. Samson," Suvi said, "when Terry says his home life is fine, he really means he suffers from economic insecurity. As we know from the data, that particular circumstance is often associated with a poor out-come."

Okay, now she'd lost me. Somehow, Suvi Singh always circled back to data and outcomes and I didn't know what else. I pictured her brain as a large vault of all the information that nobody else was interested in storing.

"He has already stolen cookies," Suvi continued, "a mere stepping stone to more serious crimes. Does that sound fine to you?"

"Um . . . not when you put it that way," Mr. Samson said.

"Terry," Jana said. "Is that why you always go around by yourself? Is that why you're a loner?"

Terry stared at Jana as if she had left her mind back in her locker.

"That's it," Jana said to Bethany. "He's one of the boys that has feelings, but he's been hiding them underneath a tough-guy mask because of his tragic life."

"Oh my gosh," Bethany said. "How many times have we seen that in a movie? The brooding loner and the girl who hates his guts, but then we find out about his tragic past and that he secretly loves the girl and would die to save her, and then she sees she

was wrong, but it's too late because he almost dies, and then when he doesn't die, they finally under-stand each other?"

What was going on? What movie was that? Why were Jana and Bethany talking to Terry Vance? Of course he was a loner—crocodiles didn't have any friends!

"That's the truth, isn't it, Terry?" Jana asked him.

She leaned over to Bethany and whispered, "He reminds me of Lance Stalwart from *Vampires Have Feelings Too*, only not as thin and pale."

Terry looked from Jana to Bethany. A crocodile smile twitched at the edge of his mouth. He shrugged and said, "Okay, you got me."

"What you need," Bethany said, "is a Belinda Swankwell. She's the only one who really understands Lance."

"Who is Belinda?" Suvi asked. "Does she go here?"

"Seriously?" Bethany asked. "Belinda is only the amazing heroine trying to cure Lance of his vampirism by listening to all his feelings in his secret cave. It's the greatest vampire show ever."

Jana nodded. "Lance Stalwart is full of feelings. That's how I know some boys have them."

Terry leaned forward, his arms folded, and stared at the floor. "If only I did have my own Belinda Swankwell," he said.

Bethany leapt to her feet. "I could be Belinda!"

With vampire-like speed, Jana pushed ahead of Bethany. Bethany staggered along behind her, and Terry disappeared into a three-person hug.

I wanted to shout, "He's not an emotional vampire! He's a Nile crocodile who has been stalking me since the first grade!" but I just sat there instead.

The rest of our time in group was consumed with discussing the various and many feelings of Lance Stalwart. Apparently, Mr. Stalwart cried if he even saw a flower crushed. He had to drink blood to survive, but he got it from a butcher and put it in a travel mug so he wouldn't have to look at it. As far as I could tell, Belinda Swankwell had her work cut out for her.

The only consolation was that Suvi, ever the scientific mind, did not see the connection between a weeping vampire and Terry Vance's cookie theft. It felt like she was sticking up for me.

When the bell rang, I staggered out into the hall, for once in my life happy to be on my way to math class.

The fifty minutes that I had just lived were almost more than I could process. On top of being terrified that I would be forced to share my feelings, which I don't even share with myself, and being on the same side of an argument as Suvi Singh, I had been violently woken up from my dream of swaggering away from Terry Vance, and he had been hugged by my future girlfriend.

* * *

That afternoon on the bus, I ignored Terry, just like I had in the morning. Only this time, I was back to ignoring him so that he wouldn't notice me. My swagger had taken a serious hit and I'd started to feel like it was last year all over again. All my summer-pool confidence had evaporated into the fall air.

"I'm losing my swagger," I said to Rory.

"What swagger?" Rory asked.

"The swagger I had at the pool!" I said. "The swagger walk and the plaid trunks and the heads-up-Snickers-coming-your-way? It's all disappearing because Vance didn't actually flunk."

"I did not know those weird plaid shorts were supposed to be swagger. I figured your mom bought them on sale and forced you to wear them."

"They're preppy casual," I said.

"They look like something a girl would wear to play tennis."

I ignored Rory's fashion advice. After all, most of his pants only grazed his ankles, and he preferred them that way because he said it kept his feet cooler. "I have to get my swagger back," I said. "I really liked it and I'm actually going to need it if I want to get Jana to like me. Do you suppose there's a way we could send Vance back to the fifth grade? Maybe it's not too late."

"Your summer swagger, if that's what it was, didn't have anything to do with Terry," Rory pointed out.

I stared at him.

Rory was not usually a fountain of sage advice, but this time I thought he might have accidentally stumbled onto something. I had swaggered all summer even though I had been wrong about Terry flunking. So what if Terry had made it to sixth grade? Until I had seen him in the hall I had been swaggering.

I could still swagger. I would just swagger when he wasn't looking.

CHAPTER FOUR

I should have seen this coming, since it happens every single year. My mom and dad wanted to know all about my first day at school. If my mom found out about group, she would have questions like: What feelings are you going to talk about in group? How do you feel about your feelings? How come you never told me about these feelings? Then, I would not only have to talk about feelings at school, but at home too. What a nightmare.

"It was the usual," I said.

My mom turned to my dad and stared at him. It was the code stare for informing him that she wished she had a daughter to share things with because boys, who then grew up to be husbands, never share anything.

My dad raised his hands in the air and said, "How is this my fault?"

My mom flipped through my schedule. I'd stuffed it at the very bottom of my backpack, but Mrs. Musselman doesn't believe in privacy for children, so she just dug it out.

"Wait a minute," she said. "What is group? Group of what?"

And here we go.

"Well," I said, trying to sound casual, "group is for . . . talking."

"Talking about what?"

"I don't know."

My mom waved my schedule at my dad. "What the heck?"

My dad shrugged. "You always say we men don't talk enough, maybe the school finally decided to do something about it."

"Seriously," my mom said, "what in the world are you talking about in this class?"

I had to tell her or she would never give up. Once my mom decides she's going to know something, she transforms into a relentless she wolf. When she goes on the hunt, we're just her helpless prey. "Well," I said, "today the Nile crocodile was suddenly turned into a great guy because he once stole a box of Thin Mints from Suvi Singh. Now the girls in my group think he's full of emotions like the guy in *Vampires Have Feelings Too*."

"What?" my mom asked.

"That's what I thought—what?" I said, glad to see that my mom shared my outrage. "How is it possible that my nemesis has suddenly been turned into a likable vampire?"

"Who is the Nile crocodile?" my dad asked.

"Terry Vance," I said. I was a little surprised he had forgotten, considering how much I talk about him.

"Oh," my mom said, "I thought Terry was the deathstalker scorpion."

"That was two years ago," I said.

"Chadwick," Mark said, "for one thing, Lance Stalwart is just an actor. He's not a real vampire. For another, you can't have a sworn enemy until you're old enough to join the military and have access to tanks and missiles."

None of that sounded right.

"The guy pushed you out of the locker room in your underwear. It was just a prank," Mark said.

That happened to be only the last prank Vance had pulled on me. We'd had gym together the year before and I always made it a point to be in the middle of a crowd while we changed clothes. It was kind of like the safety of the herd on the savannah—everybody knows it's the ones at the edges of the herd or trailing behind that get picked off.

One day, Mr. Johnson had held me after class to work on my bank shot. Why he didn't want to wait until I got taller I will never know. By the time he realized that it was totally hopeless and let me go, I was way behind everybody else. I cautiously cracked the locker room door and peered in. It was empty. Relieved, I threw off my gym uniform. Ten seconds later, Terry leapt from behind a mesh bag of basketballs and shoved me out of the locker room and into the hallway. Then he also held the door shut so I couldn't get back in. I stood there in my underwear while the nurse told me to grow up and Myra Claybrook's mom called me a creep.

Afterward, I thought of some witty replies I

might have thrown back at the ladies, like, "Is my invisibility cloak not working again?" or "Who moved the locker room?" At the time, I just stared at them like my brains had liquefied and drained out of my ears.

"That was just the last thing," I said to Mark. "There have been many, many things. Remember? My hair? The deadly sandwich?"

"Ha! The hair, that was so hilarious," Mark said.

And there was the problem with talking about the crocodile— it just reminded people about me standing around in my underwear.

Or it reminded them of my bald spots after the camping trip. Or it reminded them of me throwing up in class after I ate my whole chicken salad sandwich and then found an anonymous note taped to the bottom of my Ring Ding that said, "Your sandwich was out in the sun all morning—hahaha!" (I was sick for days.)

Every crime had been investigated but never solved. I knew who did them all, but I couldn't prove it. My mom and dad said I couldn't blame every single thing that happened to me on somebody else. They said I was getting old enough to take personal responsibility. I asked them how I was responsible for massive hair loss when all I did was shampoo my hair in a camp shower. They didn't know.

Each time something happened, everybody told me to let it go. Someday, I would let it go. I would become a wildly rich agent for NFL stars, and Terry would be an out-of-work plumber. I would drive my Porsche convertible with a Super Bowl champion in the passenger seat past his beat-up plumbing van and wave. The scales of justice would have balanced. Then I'd be happy to let it go.

* * *

The next morning on the bus, I wondered if I were actually still asleep in my bed. Early morning dreams can challenge everything you know is true about the world while still seeming totally real. Terry Vance was sitting with Jana, Carmen, and Bethany.

They were deep in conversation. Rory was near the back of the bus, but I slipped into the seat behind Jana and motioned for him to move up.

"My dad used to be the chief mechanic at the Chrysler dealership. Until the accident," the crocodile said. "A Jeep Cherokee fell off the lift and crushed all his fingers. They couldn't be fixed so they had to be surgically removed. Now my dad runs his own repair shop, but he doesn't make very much money. His whole career was wrecked."

"Terry," Bethany cried. "That's so tragic!"

"Tragic," Terry said, nodding. "That's me."

I leaned over to Rory. "Did you hear him? He's really playing up this tragic stuff."

Rory whispered, "You should've told Jana that your dad's fingers got crushed by a Lamborghini.

That would be more impressive than a Jeep. But it's probably too late now—you'd just look like you were copying Terry."

Rory was right. I should have thrown my dad in front of an expensive sports car. Then *I* would be surrounded by Jana and her friends.

"He's not anything like Lance Stalwart," I said loudly into the air.

Terry turned around and said, "What do you care what I'm like?"

"I don't care what you're like," I said. "I'm just pointing out to Jana that you're not like Lance."

Terry smiled. "Pointing it out to Jana, are you? You don't care to point it out to Carmen and Bethany? Or anybody else? Just Jana? Got it."

Got what? What did he get?

I began to get a sinking feeling that what Terry Vance had just got was that I liked Jana Sedgewick. I didn't know what he'd do with the information, but I was fairly confident that it would not involve helping me in any way.

* * *

That afternoon, as I lounged in math class, Jana's voice boomed out of the loudspeaker. "Hello," she said. "Testing one-two-three. Jana Sedgewick here. The sixth graders are in charge of planning the fall dance, so I nominated myself as chairman of the dance committee and it was seconded by Principal Grimeldi. As the duly elected chairman, I'm recruiting volunteers to help me plan the best dance ever. Meet me in the cafeteria after school to be a part of this exciting opportunity. Over and out."

Joining the dance committee had possibilities. Even if I never got up the swagger to say anything past "hey," my face would be lurking in front of Jana's face at least two times a week. The dance committee might even be considered an overlap clique. She was already seeing me in group, so this might be enough lurking for her to get so used to me that she fell into liking me.

But would it be cool for a guy to be on the dance committee? Planning a dance sounded more like a girl thing.

Then I decided that was exactly why I needed to join. There would be no guy competition whatsoever. There would be no Terry Vance hanging around like a tragic, stupid vampire. I'd be working closely together with Jana on an important project, a perfect opportunity to tiptoe to the front of the herd while nobody was looking. We might even end up with a lot of inside jokes that nobody else got. Adorable nicknames, perhaps? The Chadster? Jantastic? The possibilities were pretty endless. I felt my swagger making a comeback.

I thought I could use some backup, though. Invading the foreign land of an all-female dance committee would be a high-risk maneuver. Rory was the perfect wingman—a guy, but not a guy interested in Jana. Or a guy who girls found interesting.

I sprang the idea on Rory during lunch.

"Join the dance committee? That is totally lame!"

I knew Rory would resist, but I had come prepared to smash his arguments to pieces. "Your parents are making you do an extracurricular activity this year," I said. "What's your plan? Every single sport has a tryout. A TRYOUT. Like a test where you will be judged."

Rory looked like I had just plunged his hands into a campfire. What he had failed to mention in group was why he was so against trying out for anything. In the third grade, he had played the web in *Charlotte's Web*, the musical. First, he had stared out into the audience like he was frozen in time, which had been okay since he was the web. Then he had tipped over in a dead faint and had to be dragged offstage by his feet. He didn't even have any lines, but he said that all those eyes staring at him in the darkness of the auditorium made him feel like he was taking some kind of unholy test and if he failed he would die. The next day, he started a notebook to keep track of things that might make him faint. Tests of any kind, ranging from dental X-rays to team tryouts, were in the notebook.

"Well," he said, "planning a dance would technically fulfill my parents' outrageous demands. So wait, there's no kind of dance committee quiz, tryout, exam, speech, or essay?"

"Nope."

Rory rubbed his chin. "What about snacks?"

"Sure," I said, making a metal note to give Rory the granola bar in my backpack before he announced to Jana that he had been told there would be food.

"No to tests and yes to snacks," Rory said in a thoughtful tone.

Rory was in.

* * *

After school, the cafeteria was empty except for a group of girls at the big center table. And the Nile crocodile. Seriously? First he's getting sympathy from Jana in group, then he's sitting with her on the bus, and now he's joined her dance committee? He should be out robbing convenience stores, not getting involved in after-school activities. It was a stealth move by an apex predator.

My whole plan for dance committee was to quietly trot to the front of the herd. Now Terry was right in my way. On top of that, I would have to make sure I didn't eat anything near him or put anything in my hair. I'd have to always remember to check my chair to make sure I wasn't about to sit on something. Lurking was enough pressure—now I had to employ all my skill at evasion to make sure I didn't end up falling prey to one of Terry's pranks and looking like an idiot in front of Jana. How could I get rid of him?

The only glimmer of hope I could see was that

Suvi Singh was there, too. She had already shown herself to be a person who was not fooled by Terry and had remained unconvinced of his similarity to Lance Stalwart.

Carmen looked up from the table at me the way she does, like I'm transparent and she's looking at the wall behind me. "The chess club is in room 101," she said.

"We're here for the dance committee," I said, wondering if I should be flattered that she thought I was smart enough to play chess.

"Oh," she said, though it sounded more like, "WHY?"

Rory and I sat down.

Terry Vance caught my eye and winked. That could not be a good sign. What did it mean? I glanced at Rory, but as usual he was not paying any attention. He was smelling a spot on his shirt.

I tried to look at the crocodile without him knowing I was looking.

He winked at me again.

"Where are the snacks?" Rory whispered, having suddenly noticed the lack of a buffet.

I threw him my granola bar. Vance was sending me some kind of message. He was probably trying to scare me into leaving. I wasn't going to do it. Not this time, crocodile. I had gotten a taste of swagger over the summer, and I was doing everything I could to hang on to the last shreds of it. Jana Sedgewick, the girl of all girls, was at stake.

"Everybody," Jana said, "settle down. We have a lot to cover. First, we need to decide on a theme. We need something totally inspiring."

My whole strategy had depended on casually lurking my way to the front of the herd with a minimum of talking. Talking, as I knew from past experience, could pretty swiftly lead to saying something stupid. But now that Terry had shown up, my plan had to change. I had to take a bolder approach. Terry looked like he was about to say something about the theme, but I decided to beat him to it.

"How about *Guardians of the Galaxy*?" I said in a rush. "Or *Star Wars*? Or we could go totally retro and do *Star Trek*."

Rory gave me a thumbs-up. Jana stared at me like I had vomited in class again. This was exactly why I had planned on not talking. I had to think of something to save myself. "Or," I said, "we could play music from the Bombtastics, who I totally love."

"Who are the Bombtastics?" Suvi asked me. "What song would I know?"

I had no idea what song anybody would know, so I stared into space as if I were mulling over the Bombtastics' greatest hits before deciding on the very best one.

"The Bombtastics were *the* premier boy band," Jana said. "It was the breakup of the century and it destroyed lives."

"You don't look that destroyed," Suvi said.

"She's destroyed on the inside," Bethany said.

So, I supposed the Bombtastics wouldn't be the thing Jana and I had in common. It occurred to me that since Jana had red hair, she was probably Irish. We could bond over our love of Ireland. "How about Irish music, which is also good."

"What's Irish music?" Carmen asked.

"Well," I said, "it's music from the great country of Ireland. I think there are bagpipes involved."

Suvi looked at me like my mom sometimes does—a mix of disappointment and deep concern for the workings of my brain. "Traditional Irish music pulls from a variety of historical periods, everything from Gregorian chant to Baroque."

"I was thinking," Jana said, ignoring my bid for Irish solidarity and Suvi's history lesson, "of a Hawaiian theme."

"Hawaii is *so* romantic," Bethany said.

"We could paint a big sunset for the back of the gym," Carmen said.

"And put plastic palm trees everywhere."

"If we can get ukulele music, we can have a hula dance off with prizes."

Jana turned to Terry, who had swiveled his chair around and now stared solemnly out the window. "Terry," she said, "what do you think?"

I rolled my eyes. I was pretty sure Terry didn't even know Hawaii was a state.

Terry said, "It's a brilliant idea. It's just . . ."

"Just what, Terry?" Bethany asked.

"We had planned to take a vacation to Hawaii right before my dad's accident and we had to cancel, so the whole thing ended up doubly tragic. I will never surf the magical shores of Waikiki."

I snorted. I couldn't help myself. Like Waikiki would ever let in Terry Vance!

"Oh my gosh," Bethany said, "your dad lost all his fingers *and* you couldn't go on vacation?"

"Forgoing a vacation is not unusual in the American workforce," Suvi said, "though studies continually point out that it is detrimental to productivity. For myself, I am vigilant about scheduling time for frivolity."

What the heck was frivolity? Was it some kind of board game?

"We didn't know about Waikiki," Jana said to Terry as if Suvi and her frivolity were talking in another room, "otherwise we wouldn't have brought up such painful memories."

"It's okay," Terry said to the girls as he turned his chair to face them. "If I have any flashbacks to the day we were supposed to go, that day when our plane took off without us, I know you guys will be there to support me."

"Flashbacks!" I cried.

Everyone at the table was silent. Rory leaned over and whispered, "It's when you remember something and it's so real it's like you're reliving it."

"Technically," Suvi said, "it's a vivid memory that comes on suddenly, usually associated with trauma."

I looked around the table. I could not believe that Jana, Bethany, and Carmen were buying these stupid stories. I couldn't tell if Suvi was or not, she was too fixated on all the facts she knew. I felt like I needed to bring a rational perspective to the conversation.

"One time, my family was supposed to go to the Jersey shore and that got canceled because my brother had strep throat," I said. "I never had any flashbacks about it."

Rory nodded. "I remember that."

Jana stared at me silently. She leaned forward and said quietly, "Are you actually attempting to compare the magical sands of Waikiki to the Jersey shore?"

I was. But clearly that was a mistake. "No?" I whispered back.

The rest of the meeting was spent hammering out the details of who would do what. Suvi would shop around for prizes that were cheap, but didn't look cheap. Bethany and Carmen would find tropical decorations and make posters to put around the school. Rory and I were supposed to paint an inspiring sunset for the back of the gym. As dance committee chairman, Jana would manage the budget, decide on refreshments, and supervise the subcommittees. Just as I hoped Terry would be assigned to the subcommittee of "mop the gym floor," he nominated himself as vice chairman and Jana's personal assistant.

Why didn't I think of that? I supposed crocodiles had survived for millions of years by their cunning ability to sneak up on people. They were masters of surprise.

Jana mulled over the idea of having a vice chairman. Terry said, "Promoting me to second-in-command will help me stop thinking about my tragic life all the time."

Then he turned to me and smiled.

That's when it hit me. Vance wasn't interested in the dance committee. He had figured out on the bus that I liked Jana and this was just another one of his plans to wreck my life. He didn't even really like her; he was just using her to torture me. He had moved on from physical pranks to psychological warfare. It had started with fooling me into thinking he had flunked fifth grade. Now he had wormed his way into Jana's clique by pretending to be tragic and was getting Jana to like him. When would it end? When would his voracious appetite for vengeance ever be satisfied?

Should I run? That's what I would usually do, but

if I ran I would be running away from Jana, too. The sunlight pouring in through the cafeteria windows made her hair look like a lit match.

If I ran, I would run from all the work I did at the pool. I had spent nearly fifty dollars on frozen Snickers bars. I was closer than ever to Jana remembering my name and that she actually knew me. Could I really give all that up and go back to regular old Chadwick, a middle-of-the-herd nobody?

No, I was too close to victory. *Put your swagger pants on, Chadwick.* Fire-hair was worth fighting for.

I decided it was time to let Vance know that he couldn't scare me away this time. I put on my most grim and serious face and stared him down.

Carmen elbowed me and said, "Do you need to go to the bathroom or something?"

I looked away, but not before narrowing my eyes at Terry to send him a message—the hunted was not fleeing this time. The flamingo had reared back and flapped its wings in fight mode.

The battle for Jana Sedgewick's heart had begun.

* * *

Rory sprawled across my mom's white living room couch, throwing Cheetos in the air and trying to catch them in his mouth. We weren't even supposed to be in there, but Mark and his football buddies had taken over the den and my room was such a mess that we would have had to sit on dirty clothes. (If you sit on a pair of my used socks, you will carry the smell around with you all day. I don't know what is coming out of my feet.)

I had already pointed out that I would be blamed for the sneaker marks and orange spots on the couch because my mom said that when I had guests in the house they were my responsibility.

"That's what I love about your mom," Rory said. "It's never my fault."

"Anyway," I said, "what are we going to do about the Nile crocodile?"

"So you've totally given up calling him the assassin?"

"That was last year," I said.

"Why do we have to do anything about Terry?"

"He's pretending to like Jana to get back at me because he's figured out I like her. It's just another one of his pranks, only now he's playing with my mind instead of my stomach or my hair. He's got her totally tricked into thinking he's tragic and interesting. I'm not going to let my nemesis ruin my entire sixth-grade year by stealing my girlfriend."

"I'm pretty sure it would be news to Jana that she's your girlfriend."

"You know what I mean—my future girlfriend. We have to make Jana see that he's the same evil crocodile that he always was."

"I'll just point out," Rory said, "that your idea that Terry is the Lord of Darkness has never caught on due to lack of evidence. Even if you could prove it was him doing stuff to you every single time, the guy pulled a couple of pranks, so what? On top of that, Jana Sedgewick doesn't seem interested in you at all."

"There's tons of evidence against Vance! We both know he was responsible for the chicken salad sandwich that nearly took my life," I said.

"The note on the bottom of your Ring Ding was anonymous," Rory said. "You can't know it was him."

"What about my hair falling out? You know that was him."

"Maybe," Rory said, "but nobody ever saw him

tamper with your shampoo bottle. It could have been anybody at the campsite."

"So under your theory, you think there are random other people who are also trying to wreck my life. Not just Terry?"

"I don't know," Rory said. "I never really thought about it."

"It's just him," I said. "He's the only one playing tricks on me. Tricks that could easily go wrong and end in tragedy, like that sandwich almost did. Now, he's hanging out with Jana. He's trying to destroy my whole plan. She's supposed to keep seeing me at the dance committee meetings, which will lead to getting used to me as part of an overlap group, which will lead to getting to know me, which will lead to being interested in me. Remember? Campaign Lurk and Creep?"

"So you really feel like Jana getting to know you will lead to interest?" Rory asked. "I can't picture that."

I ignored Rory's skepticism. "First, we have to get Vance out of the way," I said. "I'm not going to keep running away from him. Not anymore. My only chance with Jana is to expose him as a fraud."

"You'll never be able to do it," Rory said. "Jana and Bethany have decided he's tragic, which makes him interesting. They've taken him on like an extra-credit project. They are going to cheer him up if it's the last thing they do. You'll never prove anything against him."

I knocked Rory's legs off the couch for the fifth time. "I'll prove the Jeep accident never happened, which unravels his whole tragic story. Like you said, if he's not tragic, he's not interesting. His dad is either missing eight fingers, or there was no falling Jeep and he is not tragic. All we have to do is get a photo of his dad's hands, *with* all the original fingers on them."

"How are we supposed to do that?" Rory said.

"It's simple. We'll find out where his dad works. Terry said he has his own auto repair shop." I grabbed my phone and Googled "auto repair Vance." For all I knew it was another one of Terry's lies, but I had to start somewhere.

"Bingo," I said. "Vance Auto Repair on Mystic Lane." I clicked on the Google map. "It's two blocks from where Terry gets off the bus. It must be right near his house. We'll follow Terry off and make up some cover story about why we're getting off at his stop. Then we'll pretend we're walking the other direction, then circle back around after Terry has gone inside. All we'll have to do is figure out which guy at the shop is Terry's dad—I'm guessing they probably look alike. Then we run up to him and get a picture of his hands and we've got the proof! What could be simpler than that?"

Rory stared at me. "That's a lot of work to prove Terry told a lie."

"It's bigger than just a lie. I'm defending justice," I said. "Somebody has to stick up for what's right. Terry Vance can't be allowed to get away with this made-up story and have Jana like him. Because that would be wrong."

"Uh, okay, Captain America."

* * *

The next day, the buses revved their engines and got ready to pull out, but there was still no sign of Terry.

"He probably has detention," Rory said.

"We've got to search the school," I said. "He's in there somewhere. Once we find him, we'll casually keep an eye on him, and if he gets on the second bus, the mission is a go."

We ran through the cafeteria, checked the detention hall, peeked into empty classrooms, and made sure he wasn't with the nurse making up another tragic story. We finally found him in the last place we looked. The library.

Either it was a sign of the apocalypse, or Terry was up to no good. There was no legitimate reason for the crocodile to be near books. I had never once seen him use his library card. The library had always been one of my safe havens from Vance. Kind of like how a flamingo might walk into the water, figuring a lion wouldn't want to get its feet wet. It gave the flamingo a break from constant high alert, and the flamingo could sit behind the last row of shelves and eat its granola bar in peace.

I motioned for Rory to go down one aisle while I went down the other. I had to find out what Vance was doing in my flamingo lake.

Terry was pulling out books and then shoving

them back on the shelves. He yanked one from the nonfiction section and said, "Absofreakinlutely."

I peered around the corner. Terry strode up to the checkout desk with a book in his hand. The librarian stared at him. Poor Ms. Bagelthorpe; I guessed she probably thought Terry was checking out a book as a ruse so he could start a fire or plant a bomb.

I motioned to Rory, and we crept along the nonfiction aisle. I scanned the shelf, looking for the space where the book had been removed. I wrote the call number on the back of my hand and raced to the computer desk.

As I typed in the number, Terry disappeared out the door.

"Well," Rory said, "we lost him again."

I stared at the computer screen. "Look at this," I said.

The call number had brought up a book called *The Psychology behind* Gaslight.

I scrolled down to the description.

The movie *Gaslight*, starring Ingrid Bergman and Charles Boyer, was released in 1944 and instantly sparked a national conversation: Was it truly possible to convince a sane individual that they were, in fact, insane? The heroine of the film is slowly and intentionally driven mad by her husband. Could that happen in real life? This book delves into the psychology of perception and how the human brain processes what it believes to be fact. It is, indeed, possible to drive a person mad, if you understand how the mind works.

I staggered to the nearest chair and collapsed into it. "Do you see what this means?" I cried. "This is about me! Terry Vance wants to drive me insane. He won't be satisfied until I'm locked up somewhere. He's taking it to a whole new level."

Rory leaned against a bookshelf. "I don't know why he needs a book for that," he said. "As far as I can tell, you're driving yourself insane."

Suvi staggered past with an armload of books. She dumped them on a table and said, "Did I hear somebody mention insanity?"

"I did. Hey," I said, pointing to the screen, "you're smart, do you know how this whole gaslight thing works?"

Suvi read through the description, nodding. "Of course," she said. "A systematic and purposeful manipulation of the psychic apparatus."

"That sounds bad," I whispered. "What does it mean?"

"In layman's terms," Suvi said, "it means that whoever checked out this book intends to disrupt and destabilize somebody else's sense of reality."

Suvi said a lot more on the subject, but most of it was like another language. She seemed to know a lot of long and obscure words. Rory's eyes had glazed over but I kept nodding to be polite.

Finally, she said, "In conclusion: blahcomplicatedwordsyoudonotknowblahblah." I had no idea what Suvi's final conclusion was, but I knew what my own was. The Nile crocodile was an evolving predator; his hunting strategies were growing in scope and sophistication. He was an evolving predator that had to be stopped by proving his dad had all his regular fingers. He had to be stopped before I got gaslighted into insanity.

* * *

Rory and I missed the second bus and had to wait an hour for Mark to pick us up. We rode home in the back of his rusty Subaru while I contemplated how to keep my sanity despite Terry Vance's plan to wrestle it away from me. Mark spent the ride advising his girlfriend on how she could improve her grade in speech class.

"You're naturally quiet," Mark said, "so that's something you'll need to overcome. You can practice by talking to me. You know, more than you usually do."

Cheryl shrugged.

"We could practice doing a debate, like I say one side of the argument and you say the other."

Cheryl twirled a hunk of her hair around her index finger and stared out the window like the Home Depot was most remarkable building she had ever seen.

I was becoming more and more convinced that Cheryl thought Mark was her Uber driver. I was always tempted to tap her on the shoulder, point at Mark, and say, "Hey, do you know that guy?"

"Like, I'll say," Mark continued, "why I think the Eagles are going to the Super Bowl this year. Then you say why you think they're gonna flame out. Your learning curve should be pretty fast; I got a B in speech last year."

Cheryl slumped in her seat and muttered, "Yay."

Mark spent a couple of minutes listing all the reasons the Eagles would go to the Super Bowl. Cheryl responded with silence. At a stoplight, Mark considered Cheryl's unusual style of mute debate. Then he said, "We could always debate *Downton Abbey*."

Cheryl twitched, which would not win any debate state championships but was a big win for Mark. I'm not sure how Mark has missed that Cheryl is not interested in his advice. Or interested in him, generally. Or even interested in being barely alive. For all his talk about how girls aren't robots, he had one sitting right next to him.

CHAPTER FIVE

At our second dance committee meet-ing, Jana gave an inspiring speech about volunteering while I watched Terry out of the corner of my eye to make sure he wasn't launching his plan to drive me insane. Jana told us that volunteers always got back more than they gave. I thought about shoveling snow off of old Mr. Swanson's driveway for him and how all I ever got was a wave from the front door. It must depend on who you volunteered for.

Finally, she said, "We can feel proud about donating our personal time to the school." Then her cheeks turned red and she stammered, "So, this thing happened. Principal Grimeldi said the rule where you can't be voted king or queen of the dance if you're on the dance committee was totally unfair and she's getting rid of it. She said nobody should be penalized for helping out. I didn't even know that was a rule so I was like, whatever, it's not like I would win."

"You could totally win," Bethany said.

"No, *you* could totally win," Jana said back.

"I'll vote for you, Jana," Terry said.

"I'll vote for you too," Bethany said.

"You guys!" Jana cried. "You are the best *ever*."

"I'll vote for you," I said to Jana.

Jana stared at me. Sometimes my timing is not very reliable. I came into that conversation way too late.

"I can't say who I'll vote for," Rory said. "I haven't even heard the campaign promises yet. Though it might be helpful for the candidates to know that I can be swayed by Cheetos."

I could always count on Rory. No matter what I did, he was always worse.

"Though Cheetos are delicious," Suvi said, "that would still constitute electoral fraud. It's not the cost of the gift but the gift itself that is concerning."

I started to wonder what went on in Suvi's house. Their dinner-table conversation must be like a meeting of Nobel prize winners.

Rory stared at Suvi. I was pretty sure he was wondering about exactly how many bags of Cheetos she might have tucked away in her kitchen cabinets.

"Anyway," Jana said. "On to business."

Jana got an update from Carmen and Bethany about the decorations. They found blow-up palm trees at a dollar store and Carmen had gone up to her attic and borrowed all the white Christmas lights. There was tons of hula music on YouTube, so Jana was going to find out if they could play the videos on a bunch of screens for the hula dance off. Suvi had shopped around for prizes and was leaning toward travel mugs from the dollar store—inexpensive, yet useful.

Jana scoffed at last year's snack offerings of potato chips and pretzels and said this year we would cater to a more sophisticated palate by offering herbed goat cheese on delicate rice crisps. That was way more sophisticated than my palate. The one time I tasted goat cheese, I thought I was eating the inside of my sock.

Jana checked her notes and said, "That's it for official duties. Terry, you were going to finish the story you were sharing over lunch before we were so rudely interrupted by the bell."

Now Jana was eating lunch with the crocodile? When did that happen? The guy was stealing my dreams!

"Right," Terry said, smiling at me, "so like I was telling you, late one afternoon last summer I see this kid pick up a dead squirrel by the side of the road. I followed him home to see what he was going to do with it. I'm thinking, c'mon, what does a person do with a dead squirrel? Was he going to give it a funeral or something? I looked over the kid's backyard fence and guess what he did? He skinned it and grilled it for dinner."

Where was this going? Why was he smiling at me?

"That is *so* disgusting," Jana said. "Who was it?"

"Well," Terry said cracking his knuckles, "I don't want to say. I'll only reveal that he has a really weird first name."

All eyes turned toward me.

"You have got to be kidding," I said.

"Chadwick *is* a pretty weird name," Carmen helpfully pointed out.

"I would not like to characterize any name as

weird," Suvi said. "However, a brief look at the most popular boys' names so far this year does indeed exclude the name Chadwick. Of course, I only memorized the top one hundred, so Chadwick could very well be number one hundred and one."

Suvi! Stop with all the reading and facts! Don't you ever sleep?

"I did not grill a squirrel for dinner," I said. "I was not wandering around the streets looking for dead animals. Jana knows I was at the pool every single day."

"I do?" Jana asked.

"I'm the candy thrower," I said.

Jana touched the bridge of her nose, right where I had hit her with the frozen Snickers. "Oh," she said, "the plaid-shorts guy."

I couldn't tell if that was a compliment or not. I said, "Rory, tell them I didn't grill a squirrel."

"Not that I saw," Rory said.

"I know what *I* saw, Musselman," Terry said. "You just didn't know anybody was looking. Why would I even make up something like that?"

"Because you're gaslighting me! You're trying to make me think I've gone crazy."

"Are you sure you need help with that?" Terry asked.

"I know what you're doing," I said, leaning toward him. "I know all about that book you checked out. I'm onto your plan and it's not going to work. I am saner than you will ever be in your whole life. My brain is rooted and glued and cemented in sanity and I am *not* going to flee like a flamingo."

"What do we think, ladies," Terry said to the girls. "Thumbs-up for he's sane and thumbs-down for he's completely unhinged."

I looked around the table. One by one I got thumbs-downs, except for Rory, who helpfully gave me two thumbs-up to try to balance the vote, and Suvi, who refused to vote at all because unhinged was not a proper psychiatric diagnosis.

So maybe I should have stopped talking before I got to the whole rooted and glued and cemented and flamingo part, but the guy was driving me to say stuff like that.

I paused. Was it working? Was I in the beginning stages of losing my mind? I might be. After all, I had just questioned if I was losing my mind, so I basically questioned my own idea of reality, which was what gaslighting was all about.

I didn't hear much of the rest of the meeting. I was too consumed with trying to analyze where the line between sanity and insanity really was. How would I know if I crossed it? Had I, even now, slipped over the edge? Would I wake up tomorrow and realize that I had moved to Thailand and was living with Principal Merriweather in a remote mountainside temple?

I only noticed the meeting was over when everybody stood up. Dazed, I followed Rory down the hall. Terry was right behind us, so we walked faster. Then Terry went faster. Then we went faster.

Terry grabbed my arm and spun me around.

Rory ran down the hall and cried, "Save yourself!"

"Listen up, *Mussel*-man," Terry said, "I'm going to drive you right over the edge. I've been just playing around all these years, but now you're really gonna pay what you owe. Got it?"

Since I was alone with an individual who probably made weekend plans to rob elderly women, I decided it was the wrong time to argue.

Terry glanced at my open backpack and snatched

at my persuasive essay, "Video Games—Fun to Do
and Good for You." "I'll just borrow this," he said. He
let go of me and strode away.

"Hey," I called after him. "You can't make me think
I'm crazy. Because I'm totally sane. I have a firm grip on
reality, and you're not going to pry me off of it."

Terry waved my paper over his head and disappeared around the corner.

Stealing my paper was a new low, but as I stood

there alone in the hallway, I began to think that the crocodile had finally made a fatal mistake in our never-ending death roll. He had Mrs. Jameston for English just like I did, and when she got two of the same paper, she would ask questions. I could prove that the research and the essay were on *my* computer. I had spent a lot of time making my case for video games, figuring I would get a good grade and then victoriously hand it to my mom as evidence of why her negative attitude about them was so wrong. If Terry handed that paper in as his, he would get busted. He might even get expelled, and then Jana would forget that he ever existed. And hopefully forget any picture she might have in her mind of me grilling a squirrel in my backyard.

I smiled. It looked like the Nile crocodile was hunting himself. When he figured it out, I hoped it would drive him insane.

* * *

"We'll go around the room so everybody has an equal chance to participate. Now, let's see," Mr. Samson said, as he scanned the list of prompt questions. "Okay, here we go—what is the one thing you wish people understood about you?"

There had to be a way out of this. I thought about mentioning I had an outbreak of flesh-eating bacteria on my legs and needed to go into isolation. Or falling to the floor into a grand mal seizure.

"I'll go first," Mr. Samson said. "When I was young and naive, I thought I would become a professor teaching at a university. After class, I would lounge at a coffee bar and have intellectual conversations with my colleagues. But here I am at a suburban elementary school. What went wrong? That question haunts my dreams. Rory? Your turn—go."

"Well," Rory said, "I guess I would like people to understand that one of the things I've recently become against is making a person say grace at the table with no warning whatsoever. Especially when a person's religious grandmother is there. It puts that person under too much pressure, and then they mess it up, and then everybody and their grandmother is like, what was that?"

That was new.

"Ridiculous, Rory," Mr. Samson said. "Chadwick?"

I felt paralyzed. My brain was experiencing a computer crash. It was throwing random messages across my mind—University! Coffee bar! Haunts! Grace! Grandmother! What was that!

"Uh, I don't like to say grace either," I mumbled.

Suvi snorted. "Deep thoughts from Rory and Chadwick."

I got the feeling I was failing group.

"Moving on," Mr. Samson said. "Terry?"

"Mr. Samson," Terry said, "unlike Chadwick, I take group very seriously. It seems to me that he refuses to talk because he's hiding a truly unstable mind. If we heard what Chadwick really thinks about all day, we would probably be psychologically scarred for life. I saw him kick a dog once."

Kick a dog? What?

Jana looked at me like she'd just smelled the dead squirrel I'd supposedly grilled.

"I never kicked a dog in my whole life!" I said.

"Right," Terry said to me with a smirk, "like you never barbecued any roadkill either."

Mr. Samson rocked back on his chair. "This is going nowhere. Next."

That was lie number two Terry had told Jana about

me. Now she thought I was some kind of squirrel-grilling, dog-kicking maniac.

I sat back. The Nile crocodile's diabolical plot suddenly revealed itself to me. There were more layers and twists and turns to it than I had originally thought. He was making *Jana* think I was nuts, knowing that would be a surefire way to make *me* nuts, thereby slowly driving me to the brink of insanity through the disdain of my future girlfriend. I was going to have to use every ounce of strength to avoid a total crack-up.

While I held on to reality with both hands, Jana turned away from me and explained to the group that she would like people to understand that cheerleading is a sport and just as important as basketball. If the cheerleaders didn't get new uniforms this year, they were going on strike. The school board would then be forced to view how pathetic a basketball game was without the cheerleaders' enthusiasm at the sidelines.

"So let me clarify," Mr. Samson said. "You want people to understand that cheerleading is a sport? Or that you're going on strike?"

"And basketball games are pathetic without cheerleaders," Jana said.

Bethany wanted people to understand that she and Jana were best friends and that Carmen was just an extra friend—a third, disposable wheel.

Suvi said, "Mr. Samson, I plan on becoming a psychiatrist. A *leading* psychiatrist known for advancing revolutionary theories and treatments. I had hoped that group would provide me with some interesting case studies, but so far that has not happened." Suvi paused and tapped her index finger against her chin. "Though your disappointed hopes and dreams might prove worthy of study."

Mr. Samson dug his hands into his thighs so hard that his fingernails turned white and I suspected his legs were bleeding underneath his slacks. I, on the other hand, began to wonder if Suvi might know something that could help me stay sane. I had known she was a superbrain, but I had not realized that she planned to be a psychiatrist. She was in the very field that could help me. I only had to figure out a way to understand what she said.

* * *

I spent all of Friday morning waiting for Mrs. Jameston to confront me and Terry about the duplicate "Video Games—Fun to Do and Good for You" essays. Nothing happened.

Over lunch, I told Rory that we needed to follow Terry home from school.

Rory said, "Terry stole your paper and he'll get caught—there's no reason to run all over the place trying to find Mr. Vance and his fingers."

"Yeah," I said. "That's what I thought too. But now I realize that we can't know when Terry will turn in that paper. He's deeply diabolical and trying to drive me insane. I can't just assume he'll make an obvious move. He might decide to turn it in near the end of the year. By then, Mrs. Jameston might have forgotten all about my paper—she might not love video games as much as we do. For all I know, Terry has stolen papers from half the school and has a whole file of them."

"He hasn't stolen any of my papers," Rory said.

"No," I said, "you could leave one of yours taped to the front doors and nobody would take it. Tell me again, what did you call your persuasive essay?"

"It's called 'Why I'm Against the Things I'm Against—A Cautionary Tale.'"

"That's what I'm talking about," I said. "Anyway, the crocodile might not turn the paper in at all. Don't you get it? He's keeping me off-balance. He's trying to get me to crack."

"Just wait and see what he does," Rory said. "If he turns in the paper, he gets caught. If he doesn't turn it in, then he stole it for nothing."

"I have to get that photo of his dad's fingers. That's the only way I can prove he's a liar. If I don't prove he's a liar, then Jana will always believe I grilled a dead squirrel for dinner and then kicked a dog."

"You didn't grill a squirrel, though, right?"

"No, I didn't," I said.

"That's good," Rory said. "You could probably get sick from eating something like that. Depending on how long it was lying in the sun. But then, you would already know that after eating the warmed-up chicken salad sandwich."

I could see that Rory was trying to get me side-tracked so I would forget to make him follow Terry with me. I had to unleash the nuclear option. "If you don't come with me," I said, "I'll shut down the kitchen."

"You can't cut off the snacks," Rory said. "Without the extra calories I get at your house, I'll get thinner and weaker, struggling to survive on greenery and seaweed crackers, until I'm just a shell of my former self."

"Exactly," I said. "But that doesn't have to happen. I have enough Cheetos and Doritos to keep you happy and healthy for the rest of your life. You only have to help me prove to Jana that Terry is a liar to keep the snacks flowing."

"Okay," Rory said. "I will agree to your extortion, but with conditions. Number one, we look for Mr. Vance one time only. Number two, you agree to back me up on the next thing I'm against."

I was fine with that. Based on last year, I was pretty sure that the next thing Rory would be against was pop quizzes. I was already against them.

Operation Flamingo Bites Back was on.

* * *

"There he is," I whispered to Rory. "He just got on the bus. Let's go."

Rory and I sat a few rows behind Terry. As usual, he was surrounded by Jana, Carmen, and Bethany.

"Why don't we go over to your house, Terry?" Carmen asked.

Thank you, Carmen! I leaned forward to hear what Terry would say. This could be the beginning of the unraveling of Terry's stupid stories. We wouldn't have to follow Terry after all—Jana would go and see for herself that Mr. Vance was walking around with all of his fingers.

Terry coughed. Then he said, "That wouldn't be a good idea. By this time of day my dad is not in a very good mood. He has arthritis because of the accident."

No! They couldn't let him dodge it so easily. I grabbed the seat in front of me and stood up. "Terry," I called. "Don't you mean it wouldn't be a good idea to go to your house because they'd see your dad wearing his regular fingers he was born with?"

Jana turned and glared at me. Terry didn't turn around, but instead said, "Did you ever get rid of that fungus? You know, the one we all freaked out about when we saw it in the locker room last year?"

"I don't have a fungus!" I said. "Stop making up all these stupid lies!"

"But the gym teacher gave you a cream for it," Terry said. "Remember? He called it athlete's foot of the groin."

Everyone in the seats around me leaned away. Jana said, "Ugh! Is it contagious?"

"I'm not sure," Terry said, "but Mr. Johnson did spray the whole locker room with bleach after he left."

"I do not have a fungus growing on me!" I said. "If I did, I would have gone to a real doctor, not the gym teacher."

"Well," Terry said, "let's hope you did."

Rory pulled me down in my seat.

* * *

We followed Terry off the bus while I mentioned, loudly, that I had never had a fungus in my life and we were getting off at this stop to go see a friend who went to private school that nobody else knew. That turned out to be totally unnecessary. Terry ignored us as he said goodbye to the girls.

They hung out the bus windows while Bethany shouted, "I hope your dad gets in a better mood! Tell him we all support him!"

Terry waved to the girls until the bus turned a corner. Then he swung around to me and Rory. "What are you looking at?"

This would have been a perfect opportunity to throw out a line like, "What I'm looking at is a big liar named Terry Vance," but I had already shaken myself up by my daring on the bus. "We're just looking at house numbers," I said.

"Absofreakinlutely, fungus man," Terry said, and strode down the street.

"Do you see what's happening?" I asked Rory. "Do you see what he's doing? Now Jana thinks I've grilled a squirrel, kicked a dog, *and* have a fungus."

"But you don't have a fungus, right?"

"Right," I muttered.

We followed Terry at a distance. He walked two blocks and then turned down another street.

"There it is: Mystic Lane," I said.

The front yards on the crocodile's street were filled with toys, aboveground swimming pools, and lawn furniture. Except for the one house that had cars parked all over the lawn. That house had a sign over a large garage. "Vance Auto Repair."

"Bingo," I said. "Let's do reconnaissance." I pointed at the pool in the yard across the street. "We'll hide behind that and scope the place out."

We jogged across the street and hid behind the pool. Rory almost collapsed it when he tried to lean against it. The water had been drained out and the sides were flimsy aluminum. I knelt and peered around the edge to Vance Auto Repair. There were a lot of broken-down cars parked everywhere, so I would have thought Mr. Vance and his crew would have been running all over the place trying to get them fixed. But there was nobody. Fifteen minutes went by and nothing happened.

"Are we going to stay here all day?" Rory asked. "I'm starving. All I'll get for dinner is some kind of vegetable casserole with yeast on top that's supposed to taste like cheese. It doesn't, by the way. I agreed to this on the condition that I get fed. If I don't eat something at your house, I won't have the strength to get up for school tomorrow and will start my slow decline. What are you going to do then? Sneak into the hospital where I'm clinging to life and put Cheetos into my IV?"

"Sooner or later, Mr. Vance will have to come out to fix one of those cars," I said. "Then we get the photo and are on our way home to the snack drawer."

At that very moment I was grabbed from behind by the shirt collar and yanked to my feet. A man turned me around and pushed me against the pool. The side buckled and I fell backward, landing in the inch of water at the bottom.

"Photo of what?" the man said. He was over six feet tall and wore a pair of overalls with a patch on the chest that said "Vance Auto Repair."

Rory was already halfway down the street.

"Save yourself!" he shouted.

CHAPTER SIX

"What are you doing creepin' around this neighborhood?" Mr. Vance asked in a gravelly voice.

"Nothing!" I said, watching Rory speed around the corner.

"Then why are you hiding?" he asked.

"We were just, well, we were . . . playing hide-and-seek," I said. Mr. Vance's face leaned down close to mine. He smelled like grease and tobacco.

"Maybe I'll call the cops and you can tell them all about it," he said.

"I'm just an innocent child!" I cried. I didn't know why I said that. I never referred to myself as a child, and it didn't seem to make much of an impression on

Mr. Vance. I doubted he would be sympathetic even if I were a newborn baby.

"You're up to no good," Mr. Vance said. "I can smell no good a mile away. Whatever it is, you're gonna take it off my street."

I scrambled up and ducked underneath Mr. Vance's arms. I jogged backward and yanked my phone out of my backpack.

He reached toward me.

Click.

"Got it," I yelled.

I raced down the street. At the corner, I looked over my shoulder. Mr. Vance stood in the middle of the street, hands on his hips, staring at me.

* * *

It took a half hour to get back to my house. If I had used the sidewalks it probably would have been fifteen minutes, but that didn't seem safe. I ran from tree to tree, haunted by the idea that Mr. Vance had

jumped in a car to hunt me down. Terry's dad struck me as the kind of person who would bury you in the backyard and then celebrate with a beer.

Rory sat on my front porch with a bag of Cheetos on his lap. Curtains hung out of one of the living room windows, so I assumed Rory had found the doors locked and decided to pry open a window and climb in. He was like a family of mice—once you got them in your house, it didn't matter how many holes you plugged up, they just found another way back inside.

"Lucky you turned up," he said. "I was just about to call your mom and let her know you were unexpectedly murdered by an auto mechanic." Rory paused and stared at my jeans. "No, you didn't."

"Didn't what?"

"Pee your pants."

"I fell in the pool."

"Good thinking. That's what I'll say if anybody asks."

I realized Rory was trying to lead my mind away from his hasty retreat from Vance Auto Repair. "Thanks for the backup," I said. "That's the second time you've yelled, 'Save yourself,' and run away in the middle of an emergency. Pretty speedily, I might add, for somebody on the decline from starvation."

Rory shrugged. "I'm against scary people."

"Everybody is against scary people," I said.

"It's in my notebook."

"Everything is in your notebook!"

"Did you get the picture?" Rory asked through

a mouthful of Cheetos. "'Cause I'm not going back there tomorrow."

"I got it," I said, pulling up the photo.

Rory leaned over my phone. The photo was a little blurry, but it was clear that Terry's dad had all his original fingers. "We'll see who's talking about falling Jeeps now," I said.

"What are you going to do with it?" Rory asked.

"I'll do a little show-and-tell in group on Monday," I said.

My swagger came surging back into me like a tidal wave. I had come up with a plan and I had successfully executed the plan. Group was supposed to be confidential, but I knew that the revelation of Terry's fraudulence would get a prime-time slot during one of Marilee's news updates on the bleachers. Group was a gold mine for Marilee and she regularly included what was said there in her briefings. Jana or Bethany would have the information to her before I even walked to my next class.

Just the day before, Marilee had heard from another group that Carol Halliday's parents were getting divorced on account of Mrs. Halliday spending their whole retirement fund on designer shoes and that Jimmy Wasseldorf's future plans included moving to Utah to get sister wives. I figured a story about a dad magically going from negative eight fingers to positive ten fingers was exactly the kind of story that Marilee would love. All I had to do was show the photo in group and let the rumor mill do the rest. With Marilee's help, I was about to jump on the croc's back and duct-tape his jaws shut.

* * *

I had spent the weekend practicing a gripping and spectacular reveal of Mr. Vance's fingers. Now, Mr. Samson looked surprised when I raised my hand to go first. "Chadwick? Okay . . ."

I stood up and pulled out my phone.

"No phones on in class," Mr. Samson said.

"I know," I said, "but this has to be an exception. I have evidence that everybody needs to see."

I opened the fuzzy photo of two hands, held it facing outward, and dramatically turned around 360 degrees. "Those hands belong to Terry's dad," I said.

"Do we see any missing fingers? No, we do not. And why? Because Mr. Vance was never involved in a tragic Jeep accident."

Terry smirked. "That ain't my dad."

"Is too your dad," I said.

"Prove it."

"It's a photo," I said triumphantly, "any court of law would admit that as solid evidence."

Suvi grabbed my phone from my hands. "First," she said, "a digital photograph generally requires the agreement of all parties before being admitted as evidence due to the risk that it has been altered. Second, this is a picture of a man's hands with no face, so how are we supposed to know whose hands they are?"

Suvi! Stop with all the knowledge!

"I saw him, Vance," I said. "Your dad has all his original fingers."

"Chadwick kicked another dog," Terry said, folding his arms.

"I never kicked even one dog," I said. "You're just trying to get me off the subject of your dad's fingers that are still attached to his hands."

"You aren't making much sense," Mr. Samson

said to me. "Fingers *are* generally attached to hands, it's part of the skeletal structure. Let's move on."

I sank down in my seat. It had seemed like such a foolproof plan. Expose Vance, then Jana would forget all about him and the squirrel and the dogs and the fungus. How could I miss that I needed his dad's face in the picture?

What could I do now? That had been my only plan to expose the crocodile.

* * *

I was getting the feeling that I was no longer welcome on the dance committee. The powers that be, meaning Jana, Bethany, and Carmen, pulled their chairs away from me. I guessed they were worried about catching the fungus. Terry stared at me with his crocodile smile.

Suvi didn't seem to notice anything unusual, but then, she was pretty busy campaigning to rename the whole event.

"I simply feel that we have no need to harken back to colonialism," she said.

What was *harken*?

"Why have a king and queen," Suvi continued, "when the history of kings and queens is replete with violence and subjugation? Why not have a top eagle instead? It honors our school mascot, more closely represents what it is we really stand for, and is gender neutral."

"This is why you joined the committee, isn't it?" Jana asked. "To get king and queen changed to top eagle."

"Yes," Suvi said. "My mom has insisted that I spend time with peers of average intelligence, so I considered how I might meet her demands while also contributing to society in some meaningful way."

"It's a little late to change everything now," Jana said. "The ballots have been printed and the king and queen nominations will be held tomorrow during lunch."

Suvi considered this and said, "Then we should at least stop referring to it as king and queen and change it to queen and king to indicate the strides we've made in women's rights. There is no reason for the male to take precedence."

"Girl power," Jana said. "I like it—queen and king it is."

Bethany held her hand up to high-five Suvi. Suvi initially appeared confused, but then seemed to remember that she had seen this sort of behavior somewhere before. She tentatively met Bethany's high five and then sat back, looking both pleased and embarrassed.

Jana began to talk about various duties to be assigned for the nominations. I decided to test the waters.

"I could help with the ballot boxes," I said.

"Terry has already volunteered," Jana said, "and he can't be expected to work with an individual who constantly insults his family."

"Not his whole family," Rory said. "Just his dad. And not even his dad's whole body, just his fingers. Though I wouldn't say he insults the fingers—he just says that they are there."

Thanks for helping, Rory.

It was decided that Bethany would help Terry, after she promised not to campaign for votes while she was on official dance-committee business.

"All right everybody," Jana said. "We all have our jobs to do. You two," she said, pointing at me and Rory, "get working on the sunset."

* * *

Rory and I rolled out craft paper on the sidewalk in front of the school. We opened the cans of paint Bethany had shoved into our hands. Yellow, red, and orange.

"How can I paint when my cleverly crafted plan to outsmart the crocodile went up in flames?" I asked. "If I even knew how to paint an inspiring sunset, which I don't, I'm too distraught."

"Distraught sounds like something a girl would get. Let's just get started and then I feel like our artistic skills will take over," Rory said, pouring yellow paint in the middle of the paper.

Despite my distraught state of mind, I grabbed a paintbrush and swirled the orange and red paint around the yellow. I remembered that Jana was counting on me. For all I knew, she might be a major art fan. If the sunset was good enough, she might be impressed. She might even begin to think to herself, could a person who painted such an inspiring sunset really have kicked two dogs?

"We have to fill the whole thing in," Rory said. "It won't look majestic if we leave white spots all over the place."

We filled in the whole paper and I used extra red as a tip of the hat to Jana's hair. But when I examined our effort, I was not convinced it was museum quality. It could either look like a sunset or look like Earth had been attacked by aliens and the planet had exploded into a yellow-and-red fireball. I cheered myself up by remembering that not all art had to look exactly like what it was supposed to be. My mom brought home a painting from a yard sale once that was just a bunch of white squares floating around in black space. She said it depicted the angst of the human condition. What Rory and I had really created was not a sunset but an *homage* to a sunset. Jana might admire that level of sophistication. After all, she liked goat cheese.

Jana strode down the sidewalk and stared down at our original interpretation of the sun setting over the shores of Waikiki. As I searched my mind for something to say that sounded knowledgeable about the arts, she said, "Start over."

* * *

The nominations for queen and king had taken the school by storm. There was no way anybody could concentrate until it was over. The dance was for the fifth and sixth grades. It was a tradition that the sixth graders threw the dance, so the queen and king had to be in that grade, but the fifth graders could vote. Boys stood around the cafeteria checking out the girls, who in turn did a lot of hair flipping and whispering and checking out of boys. Even though everybody already knew who was popular enough to get nominated, the nominations were valuable because they were solid, tangible proof of popularity.

I voted for Jana. Now I just had to find a way to let her know I voted for her, and that I didn't eat a squirrel, don't have a fungus, and didn't kick two dogs. For king, I voted for Ajay Gupta, mainly because he was one of the few popular guys who always remembered my name. I still didn't know who Rory voted for. All he would say was that it was like an insurance policy in his back pocket—if he wanted to tell the girl, he would. If he didn't, he wouldn't. If I knew who the girl was, I would warn her.

Just as I was getting comfortable in social studies and thought I might actually be able to take a nap, the loudspeaker went off.

"Chadwick Musselman, please report to Principal Grimeldi's office."

What? I never got called to the principal's office. I always flew under the radar—never bad enough to get in trouble and never good enough to get an award. On the savannah of Wayne Elementary, I lived deep in the middle of the herd with the top of my head barely visible to the falcon eyes of school officials.

Ugh, Mr. Samson had probably told the principal that I had used my phone in class. Why was this school so against technology? Didn't they understand that the world was leaving them behind? Maybe this would be a good time to try to bring Principal Grimeldi into modern times. I could explain stuff like how she should get rid of the PA system and just text everybody.

I walked down the empty halls, ignoring the kids who stared at me through the glass on the classroom doors. I supposed I shouldn't mind since that was exactly what I did when other people got called on the loudspeaker. It was always interesting to speculate on what they did to get in trouble. So this was what it felt like to be *that* guy.

The outer office was quiet, with just old Mrs. Jennings pecking at a keyboard with two fingers. She was staring at the letters like this was the first she'd heard of an alphabet. Modern times might have to wait until after she retired.

She looked up, shook her head, and waved me into the principal's office. As I passed by her desk, she muttered, "Troublemaker."

I charged into the office and said, "I had to use my phone to prove that Terry Vance's dad has all his original fingers. And, anyway, phones run our lives now, there's no use being against them. It's totally futile."

"What?" Principal Grimeldi asked.

"That's about as much sense as he ever makes," Jana said. "I'm starting to wonder if that fungus has gotten into his brain cells."

Why was Jana there?

"Have a seat, Chadwick," the principal said, ignoring Jana's speculation that I had a fungal brain.

I sat in one of the leather chairs in front of her desk. Jana paced behind me.

"I really don't know how you imagined you would not be caught. Was this some sort of prank or dare?" Principal Grimeldi asked.

"Was what a prank or dare?" I asked.

"I see," she said, in a tone that made it clear that she did not see. "Chadwick, tampering with ballot boxes is serious."

"Wait," I said. "I thought you were talking about me using my phone in class. What happened to the ballot boxes?"

"When we went to count the votes," Jana said, "there were two hundred and fifty-five votes for you, all in the same handwriting. Principal Grimeldi pulled your file and confirmed it was yours."

"But I didn't do that! Why would I do that?" I said to Principal Grimeldi. "I only voted for Jana and Ajay Gupta." I glanced at Jana to see what effect the revelation of my vote had on her. She looked like she had just thrown up in her mouth.

"Your handwriting is on all of the extra votes,"

Principal Grimeldi said. "There's really no way to talk your way out of this. You'll need to apologize to the school, Chadwick, or I will be forced to suspend you."

"I think he should get expelled," Jana said, "permanently."

I wondered if I should point out that being expelled *was* permanent. Probably not.

* * *

Despite my arguing for another half hour that Terry Vance had to be at the bottom of it, because he was always at the bottom of everything and was currently gaslighting me, Principal Grimeldi was determined that I had to apologize or go home. If I went home, not only would I get a lecture from my parents, and maybe even get grounded, I would also get a couple of weeks of advice from Mark. Over the summer, he had heard my mom complain about the state of my room and had gone on a mission to help me "get my act together." It had taken me a whole month to convince him to stop daily inspections like we had joined the army. I couldn't imagine what he would come up with for this.

I stood in front of the PA holding a piece of paper, waiting for my cue. Mrs. Jennings had paused her lightning-slow typing to turn on the power and stare at me with an expression I can only describe as glee. She wouldn't be so gleeful *after* my announcement. Principal Grimeldi had leaned over me while I wrote out what I would say, but I planned to say a few things I didn't write down.

The principal pointed at me and whispered, "You're on."

"Uh, hi. This is Chadwick Musselman. Sorry for nominating myself for dance king more than once. My apologies to the dance committee and the school."

Then I shouted, "It's not true, I've been framed! I don't know how, but Terry Vance did it!"

Principal Grimeldi shook her head. She stepped in front of the microphone and said, "That's quite enough, Chadwick. Now, on to the results for king and queen, excuse me, I mean queen and king. The nominees are, for queen: Jana Sedgewick, Tomiko Takahashi, and Lakeesha Jennings. Congratulations, ladies. And for king we have: Ajay Gupta, Jerome Smith, and Terry Vance."

I was convicted of voter fraud while Vance was nominated for dance king? It was like somebody had used a pair of scissors to shred the fabric of the universe.

Principal Grimeldi turned off the PA and looked at me with her "I am sadly disappointed" face.

Jana said, "Are you going to let him get away with that?"

The principal sighed. "Let's just move on, shall we?"

I left the office while Jana began her second bid for my permanent expulsion and Mrs. Jennings nodded enthusiastically.

The office door closed behind me and I ran straight into Skip Hammersmith, the editor of *The Eagle's Eye*. It was an unofficial school newspaper that Skip printed out of his dad's home office and handed out in the hallways. It was pretty influential, second only to *The Marilee Marksley Show*.

Skip scribbled on a piece of paper and said, "Seriously, Musselman? How did you think you'd get away with it?"

"I didn't do it," I said. "I never wanted to be king of the dance."

"Then why did you vote for yourself so much? Marilee said you voted seven thousand times. She saw it with Her Own Eyes."

"It was two hundred and fifty-five times and she did not see that with Her Own Eyes. I didn't even vote for myself once! I'm being framed."

"By who?" Skip asked.

"Terry Vance, aka the Nile crocodile," I said. "I don't know how he did it, but somehow he copied my handwriting."

"Did he have anything of yours that you had signed?" Skip asked, writing furiously.

A lightbulb went off in my mind. My video-game essay!

No, that wasn't it, that paper was typed.

"He must have," I said. "I just don't know what."

Skip looked up. "Seems like if a guy gets framed, he knows how he got framed. 'Course, criminals always claim they don't know stuff."

"I'm not a criminal!"

"Technically, you are. Principal Grimeldi convicted you." Skip whipped out his phone and took a picture of me. "Is this gang related?" he asked in a hopeful tone.

"No."

"Gotcha. Code of silence."

Skip was obsessed with gangs, though I was pretty sure we didn't have any at Wayne Elementary. If we did, they met in a top-secret location, only tagged that top-secret location, and only robbed each other.

Skip raced down the hallway with his notes.

CHAPTER SEVEN

At dinner that night, Mark looked over my head like he was peering at some far-off vista and said, "Somebody got busted because somebody forgot to consult with somebody's older brother."

My mom passed around the green beans, her opening gambit before we could have the mashed potatoes. "What are you talking about, Mark?" she asked.

"Just that sometimes, some people, some younger and less experienced people, should ask my advice," Mark said, handing the green beans to my dad without even a pause in front of his own plate.

My mom was starting to transform into her she-wolf face. I had hoped I wouldn't have to tell her about the voting frame-up, but that dream was over. "What he's talking about is—"

"He got caught nominating himself for king of the dance," Mark said. "Seven thousand times. It's all over social media." Mark patted my arm. "If you had come to me, I could have told you to disguise your handwriting."

I was pretty sure that was more of Mark's bad advice.

"Is that true, Chadwick?" my mom asked, staring at me with her piercing she-wolf eyes.

"No," I said, "it's not true. It was only two hundred and fifty-five times, and I didn't do it any of the times. I got framed by Terry Vance. Principal Grimeldi totally fell for it and made me publicly apologize."

"But why would she think you did such a thing?" my mom asked.

"Because she doesn't believe that Vance is gaslighting me."

"I thought about going for king of the dance in sixth grade," Mark said, "but I only voted for myself once. If I had decided to vote more than once, I would have changed my handwriting."

The she wolf turned to her oldest cub and said, "That's enough advice from you, mister."

"What's gaslighting?" my dad asked.

"Terry is doing all this stuff to make me think I'm crazy," I said.

My mom snorted, like she does when she thinks boys and men just don't get it. "Get over it," she said. "You people have been making me think I'm crazy for years. How do you think I feel when I find an empty milk carton in the refrigerator? Or the whole loaf of bread is gone except for the ends? Or how about when I do the laundry and there are three hundred socks and not one matching pair? Or how about when I see a box of Ring Dings still sealed, and when I pick it up it's empty because it's been opened from the back? And how many times do you think I've gotten up in the middle of the night to use the bathroom and fallen in because somebody left the seat up? A lesser woman would have cracked years ago."

I looked to my dad to see what he would say to these complaints, but he was studying his fingernails like they had just appeared on his body. I had no idea my mom was going crazy right in our own home over milk and bread and laundry. I supposed I actually did know how she felt about falling into the toilet and finding empty boxes that still looked unopened, but it was hard to remember to put the seat down and it was hard to keep Rory from devouring the Ring Dings. I guessed what made it so hard to remember was knowing that she could never find out for sure which one of us was responsible for any particular crime.

"I always put the seat down," my dad said.

"So you say," my mom answered. "One of these days I'm going to put a surveillance camera in there and find out who's doing it. Now let's get back on topic."

The conversation after that was long and filled with exchanges like: "I didn't do it." "Why do they think you did it?" "Because my name was on two hundred and fifty-five votes." "Wouldn't it be easier to just admit you did it?" "I already admitted it, to the whole school." "But you're saying you didn't do it?" "That's what I'm saying—I didn't do it."

Finally, my mom said to my dad, "If he's being wrongly accused, we need to go in and speak to Principal Grimeldi and demand a full investigation."

"No!" I cried. "Don't do that. You'll just make it worse. Remember the investigation into the chicken salad sandwich? That went nowhere, except my last name got changed to Mayo-man."

My mom's lips pressed together in a thin line. I probably shouldn't have brought up the sandwich. The investigation into the chicken salad sandwich had concluded that the anonymous note was just a harmless joke and a coincidence. Final report: the chicken salad had already gone bad before entering the school premises. The chicken salad made by my mom. My mom, condemned as the maker of bad chicken salad. For all she told me to take responsibility when something happened to me, she was still steaming over it.

My dad leaned back in his chair and chewed on the end of his unlit pipe. He had quit smoking years ago, but he still carried it around like a body part. "I concur with Chadwick," he said. "Let the boy work out his own problems."

"Oh really?" my mom said. "So would that be like the time you left him alone with a chemistry set? All by himself? And we will never get that cobalt stain out of the carpet?"

"He's not six anymore," my dad said, fumbling with his pipe. "And anyway, there's a chair over the stain so nobody can see it."

"I can see it," my mom said. "In my mind."

I didn't know why my dad sometimes got the idea that he could win one of these discussions, but hats off to him for trying. I wolfed down my dinner and left them arguing about when they were going to get new carpet.

As I lay in bed that night, I mulled over what had happened. How did Vance pull it off? How did he get my handwriting? The only thing he'd stolen from me was "Video Games—Fun to Do and Good for You." That was typed. He couldn't forge my name from typing.

Oh. No.

What was the one thing I always forgot to do? Put my name in the header. I forgot to put my name and class on the top of the essay, just like I always did! How could I forget that I forgot to do that when I *always* forget to do that? I added my name after I got to school. In black pen. That was how he forged my handwriting. All he had needed was to see how I wrote my name. That was why he had never tried to turn in that paper.

But how did he manage to stuff 255 extra votes in the ballot boxes without anybody noticing?

He'd had access to the blank ballots. He must have taken them home the night before and filled them all out. Then he had them stuffed in his pockets. When he'd walked the ballot boxes to the principal's office, he'd just shoved them in there. The only problem he would have had was distracting Bethany, which would have been easy enough. He could have just said, "Your hair looks weird," and she would have thrown her box to Terry and run into the nearest bathroom to find a mirror. And that's how *he'd* ended up nominated! He'd voted for himself just enough times, then used me as a pawn to distract people from wondering how it was possible that only weeks ago Terry Vance was a brooding loner and now he was nominated for dance king! He got to be nominated *and* drive me crazy.

The crocodile and I were engaged in a monumental battle of wits that would end in madness for one of us. As it was looking at the moment, that one of us would be me.

* * *

The article in *The Eagle's Eye* was the lead story. Skip had gotten a picture of me that looked like I was about to be run over by a car—kind of surprised and horrified at the same time.

It's Rigged!

Voter Fraud Uncovered at Wayne Elementary!

Chadwick Musselman has been accused and convicted of voter fraud during the nominations for queen and king of the fall dance. Musselman has issued conflicting statements about the incident. He initially admitted wrongdoing, and then claimed he was framed by Terry Vance, who he calls the Nile crocodile. As a journalist, I only deal in facts and am totally against speculation, but I have to speculate that Musselman may have ties to local gangs. It's a well-known fact that they make extensive use of nicknames. Nile crocodile sounds suspiciously like a name a gang would use. This entire incident could be linked to a gang war.

Stay tuned for more on this developing story and next week's exposé—"Local Gangs—Who Are They? Where Are They? What Tattoos Do They Have?"

I crumpled up my copy of *The Eagle's Eye* and casually threw it into a trash can. Hopefully, there weren't too many copies circulating. Maybe I would get lucky and find out that Skip's dad had run low on toner.

Cassie Beachman shoved past me and said, "Voter fraud? Is that really what our founding fathers fought for?"

As I searched my mind for some kind of reason why the founding fathers would be on my side, Ken Trainor stepped on my sneaker, leaned over me, and said, "Not exactly sportsmanlike."

My low toner hopes had been crushed. I could see what was happening. I was becoming the school pariah. Every school had one, and mainly it was just a roll of the dice about who got to be it. I was taking the place of Jimmy Kellerman, former pariah, who was best known for being pro runny nose and anti regular bathing.

The rest of the way to class, kids looked away or stared and laughed at me. Except for Hiram Heskell, who informed me that I was dead to him because he couldn't condone criminal activity. He planned to become a judge someday and didn't want any unsavory associates in his past coming back to haunt him.

Just yesterday, I could walk down the halls completely invisible. I was one of the anonymous middle of the herd. Now I had been driven out onto the plains to graze alone.

I slipped into the bathroom, closed the stall door, and opened my Instagram. The last photo I had posted was of me doing a backflip off the diving board at the pool. (Swagger that!) For weeks, no comments had been posted, except for my mom writing, "Wow kiddo!" and Rory writing, "Chadwick flips out," and Marilee writing, "I saw it with My Own Eyes." (I'd had to buy Marilee three frozen Snickers to get her to post that comment. One Snickers was the usual onlooker fee, another one was a consultation fee on wording, and the third one was a posting fee.) Now there were eighty-seven comments. Most of them were short, as they said things like,

"Loser!"

"Seriously?"

"Disgusting!"

Jana had written "SO Disgusting!" twice.

The only full sentence was from Jimmy Keller-man. It said, "Join the club, bonehead!"

* * *

On the bus, Rory said, "Consider it an act of loy-alty that I'm sitting next to you. Nobody likes voter fraud."

"Are you kidding me? I didn't do it—Vance framed me. That's why he stole my essay. He was never going to turn in that paper. He wanted to forge my hand-writing."

Rory let out a low whistle. "That guy is a master-mind. He goes from loner to hanging with popular girls in weeks and still finds time to frame you. A pretty meteoric rise, if you ask me."

I ignored Rory's admiration of Terry's cunning. "What am I going to do about it?"

"Do nothing," Rory answered. "It'll blow over. Remember when Susie Cotton walked around for practically an hour with the back of her skirt tucked into her underwear?"

"No."

"Exactly. It was in the second grade, but who remembers that now?"

"*You* do," I said. "Anyway, that was four years ago. I can't wait four whole years for everybody to forget about this. I need a plan to expose Terry Vance once and for all."

"You could always go to private school," Rory said. "Remember Ben Bailey? He transferred to private school and by the next day everybody was like, Ben who?"

"That's all you got?"

"I just gave you a viable option right off the top of my head," Rory said.

"Not viable," I said.

Rory's only other idea was to ask Susie Cotton to re-enact the skirt-tucked-in-underwear incident to take the focus off me.

We got to my house and raided the kitchen. "There has to be an answer," I said. "This is the United States of America. A guy doesn't just get framed and that's it, nobody does anything about it."

"That's not true," Rory said, clawing through kitchen cabinets and grazing his way through the refrigerator. "Remember that show we saw about all those guys who were wrongly convicted? Some of them were on death row."

I stared at Rory.

"So at least you're not on death row," he said, wandering into the den with a bag of Cheetos, a package of sliced ham, a Snack Pack chocolate pudding, a box of baggies, and a Yoo-hoo.

I wasn't on real death row, but I was on social death row. I had gone into sixth grade with high hopes. Terry Vance and all his stupid pranks would be left behind. I would swagger and lurk near Jana Sedgewick until she eventually realized that she liked me. It was true that I had counted on a lot of factors coming together while I was lurking near Jana, like that I would experience an extreme growth spurt, suddenly get better at sports, and develop the kind of jovial and confident personality the popular guys had. But without the crocodile watching my every move, it had all seemed possible. I would make the quantum leap from "Who's that guy?" to "Hey, Chadster and Jana—come and sit closer to Marilee on the bleachers!" Instead, Vance was gaslighting me and I had just made a public announcement admitting to voter fraud.

"If I can't figure out a way to expose him, my life is over," I said.

"Don't be so depressed, Chadwick," Rory said. "I'll stick by you. Unless the peer pressure gets too intense. Peer pressure is—"

"In your notebook," I said.

"Exactly."

"That's great," I said. "I've got one ally, except if he happens to crumble under peer pressure."

"Exactly," Rory said. "Hey, why don't you just be nice to Terry? Maybe you could give all this up and be friends? He's probably tired of it too—it's got to take up a lot of time. I mean, even if he didn't write your name on all those ballots, he knows you'll think it was him. It just goes on and on."

"Just be nice to Terry Vance?" I asked. "After years of torture, just be nice to him?"

"That's the point," Rory said. "It *has* been years. Who even knows who started the whole thing?"

I looked at Rory, dumbfounded. The guy appeared

to know nothing about my life, even though he'd been there the whole time. "The crayon?" I said.

"What crayon?" Rory asked.

"The sunset-orange crayon that I took from him?" I said. "Remember? Then he started staring at me, then he grew to an enormous size and tables were turned?"

Rory's eyes squinted like he was trying to peer into the distant past. "Wait a minute," he said. "I remember the staring and the growing. I don't remember the crayon. Are you telling me this years-and-years obsession is about a crayon? How could this all be about a stupid crayon?"

I had sometimes wondered that myself, but the endless death spiral between me and Terry was indeed about a crayon. In the first grade, I had been bigger than Terry. He hadn't scared me at all. So, that fateful day when we were all coloring pictures of turkeys and pumpkins and pilgrims for Thanksgiving, I had looked everywhere for the exact color I wanted—sunset orange. My pumpkin had to be that color. No other color would work. The only sunset-orange crayon I saw happened to be in Terry's hand.

I had boldly marched over to his desk and grabbed the crayon from him. I'm not totally sure why I didn't see that it would be a bad idea, except I was not yet known for my sense of justice. Or common sense. Or ability to realize that other kids might grow bigger than me. Or realize that they might grow bigger and have a really good memory.

The crocodile, who back then was just plain old Terry, hadn't said anything when I took the sunset-orange crayon. But his eyelid had started to twitch and he'd turned away so I couldn't see his face. I had wondered if he was going to cry and slunk back to my table with the crayon before the teacher noticed and I got in trouble.

That day, about halfway through quiet time, I began to get a squirmy "you did something wrong" kind of feeling.

I didn't like the squirmy feeling and wanted to get rid of it, so I decided to forgive myself right then and there. And also, lay full blame at our teacher's feet. I mean, what kind of first-grade teacher doesn't provide more sunset-orange crayons for that kind of project? It was pretty irresponsible.

Terry didn't blame her, though. He blamed me. He started to stare at me all the time, blaming.

I'd be eating lunch and just know that someone was watching me, and I'd look around and there he was. Staring.

I'd be swinging on the monkey bars and Rory would swing past me and whisper, "Terry is staring at you again."

One time, we were in our line to go outside, which was supposed to be in alphabetical order with me in the middle and him at the end, and I turned around and he was right behind me. Staring.

He started to really creep me out and I wished I had a time machine so I could go back and just color that stupid pumpkin purple or red. My mom wouldn't have cared—everything I made looked good to her.

While I was getting creeped out, Terry was growing. And growing and growing. I came back to school after summer vacation in the third grade and he towered over me. He sat behind me on the bus and whispered, "The tables have turned."

That year, I sat on a lot of tacks and was always

pulling off pieces of paper taped to my back that said, "Idiot."

"Seriously, Chadwick?" Rory said. "A crayon?"

"Wait a minute," I said, ignoring Rory's extremely poor memory of the turning points in my life, "*The Eagle's Eye*. I'll write an editorial and get Skip to print it. I'll present the facts like a court case. That's so much better than trying to explain to people what happened and then they are barely listening to what you say. It will give me the kind of platform I've always needed. I can explain all about what Vance has been up to. Maybe I can really get the whole Nile crocodile nickname thing going."

Rory leaned over the coffee table, filling baggies with Cheetos so he would have something to eat at his house. "But really? A crayon?" he asked.

I left Rory packing up my family's food and muttering about the crayon. I knew he would let himself out of my house just like he always lets himself into it.

I went to my dad's home office, fired up the computer, and composed my defense. It was lucky that I had already gotten experience writing "Video Games—Fun to Do and Good for You." I felt like I was a natural at persuasive writing. I laid out my case, fact by

fact, so that there could be no denying who the real villain was. Tables turned again, Señor Vance.

* * *

I cornered Skip in the hall between second and third period. I slipped him my editorial and whispered, "The scoop of a lifetime—the real, exposed truth."

Skip grabbed my arm. "You found the gangs? Where? Who? How?"

"No!" I said. "The real scoop about me and the Nile crocodile."

"Oh."

I hoped that meant Skip would run my editorial, despite his lack of enthusiasm. I needed the truth to come out fast. I practically had to run to group—it was like the whole herd had turned on me and was driving me across the plains.

I dodged Rakeesha Jones, who wanted to alert me to the fact that she had reported my act of voter fraud to the Federal Election Commission. Natalie Littman informed me that I had compromised the integrity of the queen-and-king nominations. Then she pinched me and said that compromised integrity made her really mad. I finally made it to Mr. Samson's classroom and threw myself into a chair. I had outrun them, for now.

Mr. Samson scanned his list of prompts. He said, "Right, here we go. Do you ever feel that you deserve more attention than you get?" Mr. Samson leaned back in his chair and said, "As a matter of fact I do, thank you for asking. Next."

Bethany waved at Mr. Samson.

He pointed at her and said, "Go."

"I was robbed of the nomination for queen of the fall dance. The injustice of it will haunt me for the rest of my life. I'm thinking about flunking so I can try again," she said.

"How do you feel about that?" Mr. Samson asked.

"Like I was robbed and feel like flunking," Bethany said, like she wondered how he hadn't heard her the first time.

"We should really be asking Chadwick about needing attention, Mr. Samson," Terry said. "Mr. King of the Dance here was obviously trying to get attention by voting for himself."

"Exactly," Jana said to me. "You were caught red-handed."

"No, I wasn't!"

"Seriously, Chadwick," Suvi said, "just admit why you rigged the nominations. Marilee said you were dared by your gang members. She heard it with Her Own Ears."

"She did not hear that with Her Own Ears. I have never even thought about joining a gang, and I did not stuff the ballot boxes," I said. "Vance did it. I was with Rory the whole time."

"Yup," Rory said. "Well, except for when he went to the bathroom, but that was only like five minutes."

"And BOOM!" Terry said, slamming his fist into his palm. "There you go. He had five whole minutes to stuff the ballot boxes."

"Really?" I said. "What were you doing? How come you didn't notice me putting all those votes in the boxes?"

Terry looked stumped. I should have thought of that argument in the first place.

He ran his hand through his hair and said, "I had to take a call from my mom. She was helping my dad, 'cause she's his hands now, and she couldn't figure out how to do something."

Jana glared at me. "You would really sink that low? Taking advantage of Terry supporting his mom?" she said. "That is just disgusting."

"Plus," Terry said, "yesterday Chadwick tripped an old lady who was crossing the street. She was nearly run over by a car and her knees were all scraped up. He just laughed."

"I never tripped an old lady," I shouted. "Stop gaslighting me!"

"Looks like we have feelings all over the place today," Mr. Samson said.

I stared right at Terry. "You are just making things up as you go, but it's all coming to an end. I wrote an editorial for *The Eagle's Eye* that exposes all your lies. When it comes out, everybody will know the real crocodile is you."

"You are such a bitter and spiteful person," Jana said.

Hopefully Jana would change her mind about my bitter spitefulness after she read my impassioned plea for justice. She would see that I was a nice-to-dogs-and-old-ladies, fungus-free, sane individual who would never grill a squirrel.

* * *

Twenty-four hours later, Skip was in the hall, handing out his newspaper. Kids were grabbing copies and reading it as they walked to class. I took my copy and stuffed it into my backpack, then paused and leaned against a locker so I could see everybody's expressions as the truth about Terry Vance was finally revealed to them.

"How dare you drag my name through the mud," Jana shouted at me from across the hall.

A kid I hardly knew shouldered past me and said, "My dad lost a finger in a chain-saw accident—are you saying he's a liar too?"

Bethany came up behind me and smacked me on the back of my head with a textbook. "My hair looks weird? Really?"

My impassioned plea for justice wasn't going over the way I had hoped.

I staggered into social studies and pulled the newspaper out of my backpack. What had Skip done to my editorial?

It's Rigged!

In the developing story on the rigged queen-and-king-of-the-dance nominations, this reporter has made contact with the accused. Here's what Musselman has to say in his defense:

I, Chadwick Musselman, have been wrongly convicted of stuffing the ballot boxes with votes for myself.

I was framed by Terry Vance, the Nile crocodile. (Which everyone should call him from now on, unless you like the assassin or the deathstalker scorpion better.) The evidence of MY total innocence and HIS total guilt is as follows:

FACT: Terry Vance made up the whole story about a Jeep accident and his dad losing all his fingers so he could look tragic and get Jana Sedgewick to like him. I doubt he even likes Jana, but he is obsessed with getting revenge on me. (A long story.)

FACT: Mr. Vance Sr. has the hands he was born with—eight regular fingers and two regular thumbs, equaling TEN, so there was never a falling Jeep. Here's what really happened on the fateful day of the queen-and-king nominations:

FACT: Vance used me as a pawn to distract people from wondering how he, just weeks ago known as a brooding loner, could possibly be nominated for dance king. He knew I was onto his fake story, so by framing me he gets rid of a problem, AND he gets to stuff the ballot boxes with his own name without arousing suspicion, AND he gets to try to make me go insane by making Jana think that I already am.

FACT: Vance stole my essay on why video games are

great so that he could copy my handwriting, then when he and Bethany were taking the nominations to the principal, he gets rid of Bethany by saying something like, "Your hair looks weird," and she runs to the bathroom to see what happened to it. (Nothing happened to it, it was just a ruse.) Then, when he is alone with the boxes, he puts all the fake ballots into them. Terry Vance had MOTIVE and OPPORTUNITY. FACT.

Further, just to clear up any rumors that might be going around, I have never grilled a squirrel, or kicked any dogs, or tripped any old ladies, and I don't have a fungus. These are some of the diabolical lies that Vance has made up about me. For your own safety, be careful around this individual. If you accidentally cross him, you will find yourself locked in a never-ending death spiral. FACT.

That is the huge amount of evidence and it clearly leads us to one conclusion and one conclusion only— Terry Vance, the Nile crocodile, is guilty as charged! TOTAL FACT.

I didn't get it. My editorial was flawless.

CHAPTER EIGHT

Rory walked by my seat on the bus and winked. He sat three rows behind me. I turned around to see what he was doing, but he shook his head and ducked. Halfway home, a paper airplane landed in my lap.

Tiny printing filled up the wings. "Act casual, like I'm some guy you barely know. I'll follow you like I don't know you either."

So now my own best friend was afraid to sit with me on the bus. I was probably in his notebook. I supposed this was part of the crocodile's scheme. Isolating me from Rory was just one more way to inch me to the edge of insanity.

I spent the ride home listening to Terry, Jana, and

Bethany rewrite my editorial. "FACT—it's official, he's lost his mind," Terry said.

"FACT—tell the *squirrel* nothing happened on that grill," Jana said.

"Fungus—TOTAL FACT," Bethany said.

I ran off the bus while Rory casually followed me like it was just a coincidence that we got off at the same stop. He caught up with me after the bus turned a corner. I unlocked the front door and he said, "Dude, you're not safe to be around. Hiram Heskell asked me if I was friends with the guy who committed voter fraud and then tried to exonerate himself with an editorial, and I had to say I never saw you before in my life."

"How would that even be possible?" I asked. "We've been seen together every day since kindergarten."

"I don't know," Rory said, "but he looked like he bought it."

"I was sure the editorial would prove my innocence," I said.

"Why would you say Bethany's hair looked weird? You should never say anything about a girl's hair except it looks good. Remember when your mom got that short haircut and you said, 'What happened to you?' And she cried right in front of us?"

I did remember that. There are some things you feel guilty about for the rest of your life, no matter how hard you try to forgive yourself or blame it on somebody else. That was one of them. To my credit, since then she had gotten a perm that made her look like she had been struck by lightning, but I had caught myself in time and told her she looked extremely interesting.

"Okay," I said, "the 'hair looks weird' angle was a mistake, but I was just speculating on how Terry had pulled it off." I leaned back in my chair. "I need a new plan."

"Stop with the plans!" Rory said. "Your plans make everything worse. Just give people a chance to forget about it. While we're waiting for that to happen, I'll meet you at the front of the school at lunch."

"What are we going to do there?"

"Sneak out the door and eat behind the teachers' cars. It's too dangerous to be seen with you in public."

Rory bent over his phone and started typing.

"What are you doing?" I asked.

"Googling malls. You could change schools, go wherever Ben Bailey went, and then we could meet on the weekends at malls that are really far away. People will forget you ever existed."

I felt like Rory was planning to put me into the witness-protection program.

"There's a mall in Exton, it's seventeen miles from here. We could probably find a bus to get there. I doubt we'd run into anybody we knew."

"Great," I said. "But I'd rather fix my problems than ride a bus to a far-off mall to avoid them."

"That's not very realistic," Rory said. "You've got a lot of problems to fix. Hey, did I tell you that *my* big problem is about to be over?"

"No," I said. "Wait, what big problem?"

"The kale problem," Rory said, looking at me like I was an idiot for forgetting his dire food situation.

"Your mom finally gave up the health kick?" I asked. That would be good news, as it had gotten a little frightening to go to Rory's house. There was no telling what his mom might put on the table. The last time I'd spent the night, we'd had baked eggplant with sliced tomato on top for dinner. I had thought it was a side dish, something my mom would use as an opening gambit, so I'd asked her what the dinner would be. She had looked really disappointed and whispered, "Eggplant is the dinner." She hadn't been kidding either. Eggplant was the dinner. When I got home the next day, I had to eat a whole box of Froot Loops just to recover.

"No, she's worse than ever," Rory said. "This morning, she got our hopes up by saying we were having vegetarian bacon. I thought, well, the vegetarian part isn't good, but how far wrong could you go with bacon? Guess what it was? Baked coconut flakes with some seasoning on them."

I silently gave thanks to my cereal drawer. It was comforting to know that if I had to eat at Rory's house, I could always come running home to Cap'n Crunch, Froot Loops, and Lucky Charms, my sugary old friends.

"But I don't mind the coconut flakes," Rory said, "because it turns out my dad's a genius. He's been building a new cabinet for our television in the basement. I thought that was weird because he's never built anything before. I figured he was just having some kind of breakdown from starvation."

"He wasn't?"

"No!" Rory said. "He built a secret cabinet *behind* the television. A secret cabinet for snacks." Rory rubbed his hands together. "How awesome is that? Now we can stop saying we're going to the car wash when we're really going to the Wawa to eat potato chips in the parking lot and then brush our teeth in the store bathroom. I won't have to sneak out to the driveway to get the candy bars he leaves in the back seat of the car. Me and my dad will hang out in the man cave watching sports, and everything we need will be conveniently right there. The basement stairs are creaky, so that will be like an early-warning system. If we hear her coming, we just shove everything back into the cabinet."

"Wow. Your dad has really put a lot of thought into it."

"Yeah," Rory said. "He drove me to school this morning so we could swing by Dunkin' Donuts for a real breakfast. He told me the plan while we ate a box of donut holes in the car. We're gonna pull it off the next time my mom goes for a tennis lesson. She's always gone for at least two hours, so we'll move all the food in while she's gone. My dad's calling it Mission Save Ourselves. You want to come? It should be fun—my dad said he would fill his whole trunk with stuff. I doubt it will all fit into the cabinet, so we'll have to eat a lot of it before my mom even gets home. And then hide the wrappers and brush our teeth."

"Uh, sounds good," I said.

* * *

I spent the weekend obsessively scanning all social media platforms for any mention of me—there was a lot, none of it flattering—and then just as obsessively ignoring it. On Monday, I slipped in and out of my classes with the stealth of a CIA spook. I hid out in various bathrooms, and Rory and I crept into the library and ate lunch in a lonely row of books about language. (There were whole books about adverbs. Nobody would ever look for us, or anyone, there.) As I waited for the bus that afternoon, watching Rory pretend he didn't know me, I suddenly remembered I had left my social studies homework in my locker. I ran back into the school.

The hallways had emptied out. I careened down the main hall, then hung a left. Somehow, my locker is always the farthest away from the bus line. I got the combination open and grabbed the sheet of paper. As I slammed the locker shut, I was thrown up against it.

Terry Vance whispered in my ear, "Watch it, *Mussel-man*. One more editorial and I will beat the crap out of you and blame it on the old lady you tripped."

Just then, Principal Grimeldi's voice called, "Boys? What's going on?"

Terry spun me around so that his back was against my locker. He held my shirt so I couldn't move, then grabbed my right hand and banged it against his cheek like I was hitting him. He smashed his face into the locker grill and then shoved me away.

"Principal Grimeldi," Terry said, running over to her. "I'm being bullied."

Wait. What?

Principal Grimeldi peered at the grill marks on Terry's face. "Chadwick, go to my office." She held Terry by the shoulders. "Are you all right? Maybe we should have the nurse take a look at that."

"No," Terry said. "There's no blood. This time. Chadwick's violence could have been way worse."

"My violence?" I shouted. "You were the one—"

"I'll contact your parents," she said to Terry.

"He's twice my size!" I said.

Principal Grimeldi turned to me. "Chadwick, to my office. Now."

I trudged to the principal's office. I was getting framed again. The way this was going, I wouldn't be that surprised to someday find myself in handcuffs and on my way to federal prison for some white-collar crime I didn't commit. I would be convicted of embezzlement while Terry spent the stolen money on a vacation retreat in the Bahamas.

* * *

I explained to Principal Grimeldi that Terry had staged the whole scene to frame me. He had been the one threatening me, and then when she showed up he had pretended I was beating him up. Which, if she would stop and compare our sizes, was not very realistic.

She had just shaken her head and talked about taking responsibility for one's actions while dialing my mom's cell number.

Two long hours later, Principal Grimeldi said, "As you know, Mr. and Mrs. Musselman, this is extremely serious."

"I find it hard to believe that Chadwick has been a bully," my mom said. "Further, isn't this Terry Vance the same kid who drove Principal Merriweather to flush his face in a toilet and then flee to Thailand?"

Go Mom! Tell it to her straight!

"Marilee Marksley," Principal Grimeldi muttered, staring down at her balled-up fists. She looked up at my mom and said, "That was just an unfortunate rumor. The board has assured me there was no face flushing and we have no evidence to suggest that Principal Merriweather relocated to Southeast Asia. The fact remains, Mrs. Musselman, that while Chadwick is the smaller boy, I saw what I saw. Terry sustained an injury and Chadwick did not."

"So you're saying that my son tracked down another student and started a fight?" my mom asked.

My dad snorted. "Chadwick can barely track down his own socks in the morning."

"This doesn't sound right," my mom said. "Chadwick avoids this particular kid. He calls him the angry alligator."

"The Nile crocodile," I said.

"The good news is that Chadwick will not be expelled," Principal Grimeldi said. "Your son will be suspended for one week, during which time I highly suggest you locate a good therapist. It's best to nip aggressive tendencies in the bud before they lead to permanent consequences. When he returns to school, Chadwick will be put on probation so that we may monitor his progress."

Principal Grimeldi leaned toward me and said, "Chadwick, you have made a very big mistake, but that doesn't mean you can't recover from it. It will just require some effort on your part."

It was a long ride home. My mom wasn't convinced that I had attacked Terry Vance, but she wasn't sure what to do about it. My dad said I was scrappy for taking on a much bigger kid and winning the fight. It all ended when my dad said, "Look! There's not a scratch on him! Floats like a butterfly, stings like a bee!" My mom responded by gripping the steering wheel until her knuckles turned white and asking my dad to justify violence of any kind, which he failed to do. Then they talked about the cobalt stain on the carpet.

* * *

Suspension had its high points. Most important, it gave me some decompression time from Terry Vance's mind games. Without having to constantly look over my shoulder, I realized I had been on a twenty-four-hour high alert. I slowly began to relax.

I found I liked having the house to myself, especially the kitchen. I could make myself a BLT sandwich with extra mayonnaise and minus the LT whenever I wanted. There was nobody conducting surveillance and saying, "Easy on the bacon, kiddo!" My mom called to check on me almost every hour for the first two days, so I just had to make sure I wasn't chewing when I answered the phone.

My only mistake in managing myself was the

morning I made a mug of dark roast coffee to go with my bacon-and-mayonnaise sandwich. I had been wanting to try coffee for a while and there was the Keurig machine sitting on the counter, just staring at me. It seemed like the perfect opportunity. After I drank about half the cup, my skin felt like it wanted to leap off my body and run down the street without me. I paced the house in a caffeine frenzy, opening closet doors and walking the halls until I somehow ended up in Mark's room. He calls his room the inner sanctum and I hadn't snuck in there for over a year. It looked pretty much like I remembered, as if a general of the armed forces lived there.

Everything Mark owned was in its place and lined up with military precision. His closet was organized by pants and shirts and then by color. I was looking through his books when a shelf collapsed. In my panic to get everything back the way I found it, I stumbled upon something no person should witness. My brother, Mark, the King Kong football player, wrote poetry. Worse, it wasn't even poetry about a forest or a flower like we had been forced to read in school. Every poem was titled "Cheryl."

CHERYL

Your brown eyes are like a hundred stars
Almost like you came from Mars,
Your mind is deep and impossible to know,
That's why our love will always grow.
I treasure the few words you say
Even when they are mostly "Yay."
Or your favorite word, "Whatever."
It makes me love you forever.

There was more. Cheryl was compared to various planets, the sun, the whole universe, a comet streaking across the universe, the ocean, a summer day, a winter day, a bonfire, and, for reasons only known to Mark, he'd written a poem that was meant to be sung to the theme song from *The Big Bang Theory*.

I had to wipe all of it out of my brain. I threw water in my eyes to try to unsee it. I tried to file it in the part of my brain that never remembers stuff, like putting my name on papers or putting down the toilet seat.

There was something sickening about knowing

Mark's secret life of verse, like I had peered into the deepest regions of his mind that should have stayed dark forever. Then it occurred to me that knowing it wouldn't be half as sickening as *him* knowing I knew it. I ran back to his room five times to check that I had really gotten it back to the way he'd left it.

After the coffee wore off, I started to calm down about it. After all, there were two other people living in the house. They could get blamed for reading the poems. They'd probably be the number-one suspects. I had let my dad take the rap for picking out all the marshmallows from the Lucky Charms more than once. Even if Mark realized somebody had been in the inner sanctum, there was no actual way to trace the break-in back to me.

Mark came home that afternoon and went to his room. I sat frozen in my chair, waiting for the sound of footsteps pounding down the hall. Nothing. It was a close call, but I got away with it. I vowed I would never drink coffee again. (FYI, Keurig machine—you're gonna kill somebody one of these days.)

I noticed that when you only have homework to do and don't have to sit through class, you can pretty much be done by noon. With all that free time on my hands, I supposed I couldn't be held responsible for turning on the television. Technically, we were only allowed to watch one hour of television per day during the week because my mom said that mindless television can take over your whole life. She seemed to be right, because I found a show called *Mission Almost Impossible* on the Reality 24/7 network, and within ten minutes I was totally hooked. There was a whole marathon starting with the first show and then a new episode every day at two o'clock. Fifty contestants were given an almost impossible task and then whoever couldn't do it got eliminated until there was just one winner who took home two hundred thousand dollars.

That first day I watched a full eight hours before I had to switch it off. (Binge watching—now I get it.) They were down to three people. My bet was on Hank Kraussner from Virginia, a favorite from the beginning. In the last round, they were sent to Mexico and had to eat tacos that had been marinating on a hot beach. The guy who got eliminated had dropped out in under an hour and run away shouting, "I don't care about the money, where's the toilet?" Hank just

wolfed down those tacos and held his butt closed. He was killing it.

Rory came over every day after school, sneaking in the back door. He never showed up with any good news. In group, Terry had told everybody he had been bullied. The story immediately spread through the school, mainly thanks to Jana, who had streaked through the halls like a bolt of lightning to tell Marilee Marksley. Terry was now the courageous spokesperson for a grassroots campaign to end bullying. The nickname Nile crocodile had not caught on, though half of the kids at school now called me Bullywick. The other half called me Chadbully.

My last day of suspension was on a Friday, and *Mission Almost Impossible* ended with more questions than answers. The show closed with all three contestants hanging off a cliff in the Philippines trying to get a bird's egg. If teachers put this many cliffhangers into their lesson plans, I would be on the honor roll.

I racked my brain on how I could see what happened next on the show. Maybe I could try to get suspended again? No, that was just the reality-show addict talking. Download it on my phone and somehow hide it? Probably not—Mrs. Musselman, who doesn't believe in privacy for children, checked my phone on a daily basis. Snapchat had been operational for all of three hours before it got deleted. Convince my mom to finally fix the DVR? Possibly, though I would have to make a strong case and probably throw educational value in there somewhere. It might take more creativity and cunning then I actually had, but it seemed like the most likely idea. I had to give it a shot. It would kill me if Hank won and I wasn't there to cheer him on.

Rory and I strategized my reentry into the sixth grade.

"You need to be humble," he said. "Like politicians are when they get caught lying. They just say, hey—I misspoke, sorry 'bout that. And then everybody has to forgive them because they apologized for their supposedly terrible understanding of the English language."

"But I didn't misspeak. I got framed."

"You got yourself into a feud," Rory said. "Like the Hatfields and McCoys. You can't win a feud, they just go on and on. And by the way, who feuds about a crayon? Who does that?"

Rory knew perfectly well that who does that was me and Terry Vance. He might be right about it just going on and on, but I couldn't give up the idea of winning. I had too much skin in the game to walk away now.

"Just lay low and let it blow over," Rory said. "Sooner or later, somebody else will do something weird and then the whole school will be talking about them instead of you."

"Everybody is *still* talking about me?"

"Well, it's hard not to, what with your face being on the S.A.B. flyers."

"The what?"

"The Students Against Bullying flyers," Rory said. "It's turned into a real movement."

* * *

My mom leaned on the kitchen counter. "I'm sure you'll be happy to get back to school. And your arteries will be happy to get off the bacon."

I hadn't been aware that my mom had been monitoring the bacon situation. There wasn't much you could get past her—I wondered if leaving the pan in the sink had tipped her off. To get her mind off it, I said, "I've been meaning to mention, I really believe it's time we got the DVR fixed, or if not, then we should just get a new one. I hear they're very inexpensive these days."

I held my breath and watched how that announcement would fly.

"Why do you need a DVR?"

And here we go. I was about to give the speech of a lifetime. I took a deep breath and said, "There's so much culture on during the day. But before I talk about the amazing culture, I will point out that I only know that because I only watched one hour of it and then did not watch one hour at night so didn't break any house rules. Now, back to the culture—"

"What show were you watching?" she asked, spraying down the counter and wiping it with a paper towel. She furiously scrubbed at the purple Kool-Aid stain that we all knew was never going to come out.

"Uh, it's a show called *Mission Almost Impossible*," I said. "What it's really about is mental discipline and overcoming the odds, which I think is a great example to me as a youth in my formative years."

My mom put down the spray bottle. "Is this some kind of reality show?"

"It is, in fact, real," I said smoothly. "Just as documentaries are real, which we can all agree are highly educational."

"Chadwick, don't be ridiculous."

"You wouldn't say that if you had seen Hank hanging by his fingernails from a cliff in the Philippines!"

Mark had walked into the kitchen. He opened the refrigerator and drank milk out of the carton while my mom had her back to him. He pointed the carton at me. "Sitting home watching reality shows is not cool. Grandma does that," he said. "Remember how she got obsessed with *Love Is in the Air*? She just gave up trying to be a contestant last year. Very uncool, Chadwick."

"Oh really?" I said. "Well, poetry is uncool also." (That was a mistake, because now I had connected myself to the inner sanctum break-in.)

Mark whipped his head around and stared at me. I looked out the window like I had never said anything.

"No bickering," my mom said.

I heard the front door slam. My dad came in and eyed my mom with the spray bottle in one hand and paper towel in the other. He casually slid his briefcase over the purple stain on the counter. "Wow," he said, looking everywhere but the counter, "the place looks great."

We had all gotten into the habit of trying to cover

up the purple stain after my dad told us it made my mom talk about getting new counters that we couldn't afford. My dad always complimented the look of the room as a distraction maneuver.

My mom used her spray bottle to slide my dad's briefcase back in his direction. She stared down at the purple stain and said, "It's still there."

I got my dad his after-work Diet Mountain Dew so he could relax. Then I tried to make my case to him about the importance of finding out who would win *Mission Almost Impossible*. Once I started talking about the actual challenges, he started to get really interested.

"It's a reality show," my mom said, as if reality shows were some species of highly dangerous animal.

"What's the prize?" he asked me, casually sliding his briefcase back over the purple stain.

"Two hundred thousand dollars," I said.

"It's a reality show," my mom said again, staring down at his briefcase.

"Well, I for one would like to know if Hank claims victory," my dad said to my mom. "It also occurs to me that if we finally fixed the DVR, I could record football like I used to. That way, if I get dragged to your mother's house for Sunday dinner, I won't miss the game."

"*Dragged* to my mother's?" my mom asked.

I backed out of the room and left my dad to it. In about a half hour, they would land on the conversation about the Kool-Aid stain and new counters. My dreams of a DVR were over.

* * *

My first post-suspension bus ride did not go how I thought it would, but I supposed I had been overly optimistic when I imagined I would get the silent treatment.

Jana said to Rory, "Friends don't let friends bully."

"Just say no to bullying," Bethany called.

"Hey, Chadwick," Carmen said, "did you know that bullies are really cowards?"

The rest of the kids on the bus turned to see if I did know that while gravely shaking their heads.

It was hard to believe that anyone could look at me and think *bully who pushed a kid's face into a locker grill*. Rory and I had never even thought of throwing punches at each other. Both of us were terrified of getting hit in the face. The last time I had a physical fight was in kindergarten, over who had the right to water the lima beans on the windowsill. I got clocked by Mary Henswell and went home crying.

I had to report to the principal's office before I could go back to class. Mrs. Jennings waved me in with a smirk. As I walked by her desk, I glanced down at her keyboard, as if to say, "Still searching for that elusive letter?"

"It's good to see you, Chadwick," Principal Grimeldi said. "I trust you've taken the past week to reflect on your actions."

I figured the principal would not be impressed to find out that I had spent my suspension week watching a reality show, eating a pound of bacon, freaking out on caffeine, and trying to unsee Mark's love poems, so I said, "Yeah, I've done a lot of reflecting."

"And I hope your parents have located a therapist by now?"

I had forgotten they were supposed to do that. I didn't want my mom and dad to get in trouble for not getting me help, so I said, "Uh-huh. Dr. Silverstein is great." Hopefully, she wouldn't find out that Dr. Silverstein was my dentist.

"Excellent. And have you brought the letter of apology you were to write to Terry?"

I reached into my backpack. I hoped my apology would get by her—I was pretty sure she expected something longer. But to be fair to myself, I really couldn't be expected to write a whole novel for a crime I didn't even commit.

Principal Grimeldi unfolded the paper.

Sorry dude.

"That is not sufficient," she said, pushing the paper back to me. "At least one paragraph, please. Bring it with you to our next meeting."

"Can it be a short paragraph?" I asked. "Technically, a paragraph could be one sentence."

"Make it a proper apology, no matter how many sentences it takes," she said. "Now, I planned to change your schedule, as you and Terry are in the same group. However, I thought it over and decided that tensions between you probably won't be resolved by avoiding each other and the best venue for talking is group, after all. Terry is agreeable; in fact, he has handled this situation with surprising grace. But I must stress that you are not to display any aggression toward Terry or in any way make him uncomfortable. Do I have your word?"

I couldn't believe it. While I was kicking back, watching a reality show with a plate of bacon on my lap, Terry had been busy brainwashing the principal. I should have known that when you're in a hundred-years' war with a crocodile, there's no such thing as a day off.

"Absolutely," I said.

CHAPTER NINE

Mr. Samson said, "And the question of the day is: What has been the most traumatic event of your life? I'll go—six years ago, I proposed to my girlfriend. She stared at me down on one knee and said, 'You can't expect me to marry an elementary school teacher. I mean, what kind of vacations could we afford? And look at the size of that ring. You'd need a magnifying glass just to show it to people.'"

Mr. Samson looked off into the distance and said, "It was at that moment when I realized she wasn't madly in love with me, like I thought. She married a chiropractor three months later. They're probably vacationing in the Caribbean as we speak. Who's next? Yes, Bethany?"

"Robbed."

"Are you talking about the nominations again?"

"Yup."

"Anything else you want to say about it?"

"Nope."

"Righty then," Mr. Samson said. "Jana?"

"Mr. Samson," Jana said, "I am no stranger to trauma. Only yesterday I realized that, although I have worked tirelessly, nobody has thanked me for all my efforts to make our dance the best fall dance ever. No, they are all just going to go and enjoy it without a thought as to what actually goes into planning such an event. I am not asking to be thanked, but a thank-you would be nice."

Mr. Samson sighed. "Thank you very much for planning the dance, Jana. It will be the highlight of my social season. Your turn, Chadwick."

I had already prepared what I was going to say to make sure it was good. Since I was probably on my way to failing Spanish, I couldn't afford to fail group too. One class that went bad would be easy to explain to my parents. I would go with the tried-and-true "the teacher hates me" explanation. I had already prepared what I was going to say about Spanish, "*el profesor me odia*," figuring that saying it actually in the language would make it more believable. But two teachers hating me would be harder to pull off. That would be the kind of thing where my mom would say, "Two teachers hate you? I better go talk to the principal about all your hateful teachers." Then the truth would come out—my Spanish teacher didn't hate me, she just hated my inability to speak Spanish.

"Besides being framed for two crimes I didn't commit," I said, staring at Terry, "I've been traumatized by amateur love poems. I've done everything I can to unsee them but they are burned into my brain and will remain a haunting memory until I'm old enough to be senile."

Mr. Samson held his hands up. "I'm not even going to ask what that means."

"It means he's becoming seriously delusional, Mr. Samson," Terry said. "At this point, you've done all you can—he needs professional help."

"What I need," I said, "is a professional bodyguard who can take out any deranged person who can never let go of one thing for years and years."

Terry didn't even flinch. He just sat back and smiled at Jana.

After group, Suvi stopped me in the hall. "What is up with you?" she asked. "First bullying, and now you're afraid of poems? Marilee said she saw with Her Own Eyes that you were going to rob Terry for your gang—was it for drug money?"

I was getting a little tired of Marilee Marksley's eyes. "Marilee's eyes were not even in that hallway unless they can now jump out of her eye sockets and were rolling around on the floor by themselves," I said. "Terry totally framed me. He held himself against my locker like I was beating him up, but I'm not a bully! I don't want to fight anybody. Terry keeps framing me for stuff because I know the real truth about his dad, which unravels all his lies. He's nothing like Lance Stalwart—you see that, right?"

Suvi glanced at a S.A.B. flyer someone had taped to the wall.

"The poems are a whole other story that has nothing to do with it," I said, it now having occurred to me that revealing I had been traumatized by poems might not have sounded totally rational without knowing the whole situation. "Look, how is it possible that if I was chasing Terry down, we ended up at *my* locker?" I paused and wondered why I hadn't thought of that before. How come Principal Grimeldi had failed to notice that fact?

"Maybe," Suvi said, looking thoughtful. "I've been a little suspicious about something Terry said. I told my mom and dad about the Jeep accident and they said they'd never heard of that happening, even though they've both worked at the hospital for years. My mom thought that was strange because they always talk about the interesting cases over lunch. She said, if somebody came in with eight crushed fingers, it would still be a hot topic at lunch."

"See!" I said. "Finally, somebody else gets that he's lying!"

"So, you weren't trying to rob Terry for drug money?"

"No!"

"And you're not delusional about poetry? I mean, delusional in the clinical sense, not the name-calling sense?"

"No, but Vance has been gaslighting me. You know, trying to make me go insane. Who knows what I'm getting delusional about."

"So you think he's done it?" Suvi asked, looking at me with a critical eye.

"I can't tell," I said. "It's hard to be totally positive one way or the other."

"Hmmm," Suvi said. "This is the first decent psychological problem I've seen. Especially if you actually *have* gone insane. Maybe I could evaluate you; it would be good practice for my career."

I wasn't so sure I wanted to be evaluated by Suvi Singh. What if it came out bad? Her parents were doctors, who knew what they might do about it.

"I could do it after school," she said. "But you'd have to wait until four thirty. I always watch *Mission Almost Impossible* as soon as I get home. Usually it would be later, but I'm done with dance committee. I've accomplished all that I can there."

Suvi watched *Mission Almost Impossible*? If I let her evaluate me, I might actually get to see how Hank from Virginia was doing? "I love that show. It's reality television at its finest," I said.

Suvi stretched herself taller and leaned over me. Suddenly, she didn't look so friendly. "Are you mocking me? Is a highly intelligent person never supposed to relax via commonplace activities the average American finds entertaining? Do you have opinions on that, foreigner?"

"What?" I said. "No. I don't have any foreign opinions."

Suvi kept staring at me.

"Seriously. I'm rooting for Hank, I'm pretty sure he's going to take home the prize."

"No way," Suvi said. "Barb from Vegas has it wrapped up."

"She's pretty good, but Hank is stronger and the challenges are getting harder."

"We'll see who gets the first bird's egg."

"*Could* I see it?" I asked, my voice sounding full of the hope of a reality-show addict who had been denied access.

Suvi thought for a moment. Then she said, "You can come over and watch it if you want. But only if you don't talk over the show. If you talk over the show—you'll get deported right out the front door. After it's over, I'll do a psychological workup on you."

"I won't talk over the show. I swear."

* * *

Suvi only lived six blocks from me. I never saw her on the bus because I was on the number twelve and she was on the number eleven, but sometimes I saw her at the pool or the park. Up until now, I had steered clear of her because of her extreme smartness, though I never said that out loud to anyone except Rory. I had said it in front of my mom once and then had to listen to an hour-long lecture on women's rights. I'm all for women's rights so I finally told my mom that I was too stupid to hang with Suvi because I was a guy. She seemed satisfied with that explanation.

I felt like I should bring Rory with me to Suvi's house. Even though it was only Suvi, technically she was a girl. I had never set foot inside a girl's house and there might be all kinds of rituals I knew nothing about. No matter how badly I stumbled through something, Rory could be counted on to do something worse and make me seem not that bad. Then, when I was being mentally evaluated, Rory could defend me if some of my answers seemed strange. He knew my whole history and could provide crucial explanations for anything I did or said that didn't sound totally rational. That is, if he could bother to remember the details of my life. I still couldn't get over that the sunset-orange crayon of first grade was news to him.

"I don't want to watch a reality show and sit in on a psychiatric session," Rory said. "I want to be at your house having snacks, like we always do."

"You think you don't want to watch the show," I said, "but that's just because you didn't see Hank hanging from a cliff in the Philippines. Being mentally evaluated is a small price to pay to find out what happens. Anyway, Vance has been riding me pretty hard these past couple of weeks and it wouldn't hurt to get a professional opinion to find out if I'm cracking under the pressure."

"You cracked a long time ago," Rory said. "You don't need Suvi to tell you that. Why can't we just watch the show at your house?" he asked. "I mean, Suvi is, you know . . ."

"Scary. I know. But we can't watch it at my house—no DVR."

"I have a DVR. We could record it tomorrow and watch it at my house," Rory said.

"Your mom makes us drink kale smoothies," I pointed out.

"I know! I've told her a million times that I'm

against them. They're in my notebook with five stars next to them—my highest rating for things I'm against. But she just acts like I didn't say anything and starts the blender."

"Your house is out until your dad pulls off Mission Save Ourselves," I said.

Rory groaned. "He's getting nervous about it. We were all set for a go, and then my mom canceled her tennis lesson this week. She says she has a sore elbow, but my dad is wondering if she knows something is up. He's all fidgety around her and keeps chasing her around trying to rub Bengay on her elbow. We'll see if she cancels next week's lesson."

"As I said, your house is out. Listen, if we just stick to talking about the show, Suvi won't be that scary. It's only when you talk to her about science and facts that you're lost in five minutes and feel yourself going down the drain. If she starts talking about data and you don't understand what she's saying, just nod—that's what I do. All you have to do is defend me while she's doing my evaluation. You know, if it starts to look like she's getting suspicious about my sanity."

"How am I supposed to defend your sanity?"

"If she starts talking about any kind of diagnosis,

you can change the subject and tell her about all the things you're against."

"Do you think she'd be interested in what I'm against?" Rory asked, clearly finding the idea intriguing.

"Probably," I said, hoping to lure Rory on. "I mean, I'm used to your notebook, but it would be all brand-new to Suvi."

* * *

We knocked on Suvi's door while I held on to Rory's shirt collar so he couldn't have second thoughts. It would be just like him to make a run for it, yell "Save yourself," break into my house, and eat everything in the kitchen.

"Hey," Suvi said as she opened the door. She glanced at Rory. "You're a *Mission Almost Impossible* fan too?"

"Um, actually," Rory said, "I've never seen it. But Chadwick says it's great."

"You have no idea," Suvi said.

We went into the living room. Just as I had

suspected, Suvi's house was overflowing with knowledge. There was a whole wall of bookshelves full of serious-looking books and a pile of magazines about architecture and medicine. In my house, we only got *People*. No wonder I couldn't understand half of what Suvi said. I never had a fighting chance.

I noticed a large bowl of potato chips on the coffee table—it was almost like Suvi had known I would bring Rory with me. He ran toward them with his hands out like a zombie chasing human flesh. I hoped she didn't actually want any of the chips—she would never be able to get to them in time.

"Here we go," Suvi said.

Mission Almost Impossible was riveting. All three contestants were still on the cliff in the Philippines, desperately trying to get a bird's egg. Hank from Virginia slipped and if it weren't for his harness, he would have plummeted to a bloody death. He swung helplessly, banging into the side of the mountain.

Your average guy would have given up, but Hank grabbed a ledge, swung a leg up, and reached forward. He held a bird's egg over his head, victorious. Barb from Vegas was right behind him. Jeremy from Nebraska got an egg before Barb, but he broke it and got disqualified. He was going back to the Midwest with egg literally on his face.

Rory sat back and said, "This show is awesome."

"I know, right?" Suvi said, shutting off the DVR. "What kind of people would risk their lives on a television show? As a medical professional, it's these kinds of questions that keep me up at night."

"Those people are nuts!" Rory said.

"It really isn't appropriate, or accurate, to call somebody nuts," Suvi said to Rory, "but I suppose I can't blame you for not knowing. Another thing you should know is that usually a doctor and her patient would speak privately. There might be all sorts of things Chadwick wants to reveal during our session that would be embarrassing or against the law. Confidentiality is everything."

"Rory already knows everything about me," I said, "At least, everything he bothers to remember. He can explain anything you think might not be totally normal."

Suvi nodded. "Very well, we will begin."

I sat still in my chair, feeling like I didn't know how to act while I was being evaluated. If I leaned back and looked casual, did that say something? If I sat up straight, did that say something? What did normal look like? Why hadn't I paid attention to how I sat before Vance began driving me insane so I could copy it now?

"What do you feel is your biggest problem?" Suvi asked.

That one was easy. I had been wrestling with the same big problem for most of my life. "It's not a what, it's a who. Terry Vance," I said. "He's my biggest problem. I call him the Nile crocodile. Except last year I called him the assassin. And then other years there were other names. The viper, the deathstalker scorpion, stuff like that . . ."

Suvi was silent and staring, neither approving nor disapproving of what I said. I looked to Rory for help, but he was licking his finger and rubbing it around the empty bowl of potato chips to get the last of the salt.

Suvi finally broke the silence and said, "And why do you think Terry Vance is a problem for you?"

"I told you how he framed me for voting for myself as dance king and he framed me for bullying him and he's gaslighting me."

"You were speaking to Suvi at that time, not me."

"Um . . . who am I speaking to now?" I asked.

"Dr. Singh," she said. "If I am going to evaluate you, I have to maintain professional distance. Now, tell me more about what has been happening to you."

"Okay," I said, "remember in the library when I showed you, I mean, I showed Suvi, that description of a book about the movie *Gaslight*? Then you said all kinds of stuff I couldn't understand. Terry checked out that book—it explains the whole psychology of gaslighting. He's using the techniques to make me crazy, but I'm really sane, just like the lady in the movie. At least, I hope so. That's why he framed me for voter fraud and then framed me for bullying and told everybody I grill squirrels and kick dogs and trip old ladies and have a fungus. He's trying to make Jana think I'm insane, which is the one thing he knows would be guaranteed to make me insane."

"And do you do those things?" Suvi asked. "Do you grill squirrels and kick dogs and trip old ladies? Do not be ashamed to admit it—the important thing is that you are here, asking for help."

"I never did any of those things! I'm a nice person.

I really am. At least, I'm pretty sure that I am. Rory? I'm nice, right?"

Rory didn't answer, which was not surprising since he now had his face inside the potato-chip bowl so he could lick out the salt more efficiently.

"Tell me more of Jana," Suvi said. "If it is true that you would, indeed, go insane if *she* thought you were insane, she must be an important figure in your life. How do you feel about her?"

"Well, I mean, she's Jana Sedgewick," I said.

"Try and be specific," Suvi said. "What qualities does she possess that you find so compelling?"

"Um, she's the girl of all girls. That's obvious."

"Obvious to you, perhaps," Suvi said. "But why? What makes her the girl of all girls?"

"Well," I said, "I like her hair. It's red. There are different shades of red and hers is really dark red, which I think looks great. In the sun, it almost looks like her skull is on fire. Also, I smelled it once and it smelled like grass."

Rory snorted from inside the chip bowl.

Suvi nodded as she took notes. "What else? Besides her hair?"

"Besides her hair? Well, there would be, that she's popular. That's good, right?"

"Her hair and her social standing," Suvi said. "What else?"

What else? I searched my brain for what else. Her hair was great and she was popular. What else? It was

Jana Sedgewick—there were a million things to like. What were they?

It began to dawn on me that I didn't know what those other million things were. "Uh . . . I think that's it, actually," I said.

"So, let me see if I understand you correctly," Suvi said, reviewing her notes. "Your biggest problem is Terry Vance, who is trying to make a red-haired popular girl think you are insane, thereby driving you insane."

That pretty much summed it up, though it didn't sound so logical when Suvi said it.

"Chadwick, I believe you need to clarify your goals," Suvi said. "What is it you really want?"

What did I really want? Did I really want Jana to be my girlfriend just because she was popular and had red hair? When I fell for Jana last year, I didn't actually know her. It had just seemed important to be part of a power couple; so many other kids were doing it. I had looked around for somebody and noticed her hair. After that, I would go to basketball games and pretend to care who won, but really just watch her cheer and swing her hair all over the place. Then I started to think about her hair when she wasn't even around. That had seemed like a sign that we should be a couple.

Jana was at the front of the herd and I was shuffling along in the middle, slowly lurking and creeping my way forward. Along the way, I had filled in all these great personality traits that I kind of assumed she had, because she was at the front of the herd. I mean, how else could she have gotten there? But once I got close enough to know her, I noticed that she was more complicated than I would have thought. And sometimes a little scary.

And here was Suvi, pretty complicated and scary herself. Were they all like that? It would make having a popular girlfriend harder than I'd thought. It would make having *any* girlfriend harder than I'd thought.

But what about Cheryl? All girls couldn't be complicated and scary. Mark's girlfriend wasn't.

I paused. Nobody actually knew what Cheryl thought about. She could be thinking about murdering us in our beds for all Mark knew about it.

Being a part of a couple felt a lot more complicated than just sitting together at lunch, now that I was viewing it up close.

"I can't be totally sure," I said to Suvi, "but maybe I don't have the crush on Jana that I thought I did."

Suvi nodded and smiled as if I'd had some kind of breakthrough in my therapy. "You were never in love with Jana in the first place," Suvi said. "You were in love with a person you created in your imagination."

Dr. Singh was good. Very good.

"Since you have gained further insight into your feelings, how has your view of Terry changed?" Suvi asked. "Will he still able to drive you insane by making Jana think you are insane?"

"Probably not," I said, "but he'll just think of something else. He always thinks of something else."

"I see. Terry will remain an ongoing issue for you to confront and work through. What strategies have you employed to solve your problem with your classmate?" Suvi asked, chewing on the end of her pencil.

"Mainly running for my life," I said.

"And running for your life has not proved successful. Is there anything else you might do?"

"I don't know," I said. "Lately, I've been standing up to him, but so far that's not getting me anywhere either."

"What do you do to stand up to him?"

"I tell him to stop gaslighting me," I said. "And I wrote a scathing editorial for *The Eagle's Eye*."

"And what else?"

"Uh, that's it."

"No wonder you are not getting anywhere, Chadwick. An eye for an eye, a tooth for a tooth," Suvi said. "If Terry is gaslighting you, then you have to gaslight him back."

"Oh," I said. "That's not what I thought a doctor would say."

"Of course not," Suvi said. "You are now talking to Suvi, not Dr. Singh. The doctor would never recommend such a step. It would be completely irresponsible and she'd get her license revoked."

"But you, as Suvi, think I should gaslight him back?"

"Well," she said, "are you a mouse or a man?"

A mouse or a man? Suvi was asking me about my swagger! Did I shiver like a mouse or swagger like a man?

But gaslight Vance back? Could it even be done? Could I be as devious and cunning as the Nile crocodile?

"I believe we will leave our session there," Dr. Singh said. "It's time for you to do some private reflecting on what we have discussed. Ask yourself, who do I—Chadwick Musselman—really want to be? A mouse? A man? Do not jump to a conclusion too quickly or judge your natural inclinations. After all, there is no shame in mouse-hood. Or at least, there shouldn't be. We can continue our session tomorrow."

"Can me and the mouse come early to watch the show?" Rory asked.

"Sure," she said.

"And maybe you could supersize the bowl of chips?" Rory said. "Or add a bowl of Cheetos? Either way works for me."

* * *

On the way home, I said, "What do you think about what Suvi said?"

"Which thing?" Rory asked.

"About whether I'm a mouse or a man. About how

if I'm not going to be a mouse, I have to go for an eye for an eye. She thinks I should gaslight Terry back."

"I wouldn't try it, it sounds complicated," Rory said. "Just be mouse and apologize to Terry. Hey! Why don't you buy him a crayon as a replacement for the one you stole? He'd totally have to forgive you and the whole thing would be over."

"It's years too late for that," I said.

"No, it isn't. My mom says it's never too late to admit you're wrong. Only last week, my dad finally admitted he was the one who washed her white shirt with his red shirt, making her shirt pink. That was two years ago, but she just stayed with it until he apologized."

"Let me guess—and then she made him drink a kale smoothie to pay for his crime," I said.

"No," Rory said, "a beet and banana smoothie. It was pink, get it? He'll never touch her laundry again. So, what do you think? Go get that crayon and we can forget all about Terry."

Rory followed me home, listing all the ways I could return Terry's crayon. The last one I heard had something to do with slipping it onto his lunch tray inside a heartfelt Hallmark greeting card.

He conveniently followed me into the house because he knew it was pizza night. Rory hadn't missed a pizza night at my house in years, whether he was invited or not.

We sat at the dinner table, waiting for the doorbell to ring. Mark sat across from us with a look of steely determination. Once the pizza arrived it would be every man for himself. While I waited, I weighed the opposing views of Suvi and Rory. Suvi thought I should go on the offensive and Rory thought I should give Terry back his crayon. What did I think?

I'd known Rory a lot longer, so I should probably trust him more. But then, Suvi's idea was bold. It was like my therapist had the heart of a lion. There was something liberating about her idea. But also something dangerous. I had tried fighting back in fourth grade and experienced the viciousness of a cornered crocodile. If I gaslighted him back, he might just get madder. Then what would he do?

"Mark," I said, "what do you think is best—going on the offense or staying on defense?"

"I'm a quarterback," Mark said. "I count on them both."

"I know, but just in general," I said.

"Well," Mark said, looking pretty pleased that I had asked for his opinion. "If you want to win, you better have a good offense."

I sat back. I had been playing the game with the crocodile all wrong. I had given up on offense after trying it only once in the fourth grade. I should have kept going. That was the only way to win. A gazelle could only hide in the middle of the herd for so long. Sooner or later, it fell behind or accidentally ended up at the edges. There was only ever one ending to the gazelle's story, and it was not winning.

"Chadwick," my mom said, laying out napkins, "you know I would never want to stomp on your dreams, but football is not your sport, honey. You'd get trampled and end up with a head injury. Let's think about tennis."

I nodded and kept thinking. Terry was always on the offense. Year by year, his plays had become more devious. In second grade, I had sat on a lot of tacks, by third grade he was giving me food poisoning, by fourth grade my hair was falling out, by fifth grade I was standing in the hall in my underwear. Now he was running an elaborate scheme to make me lose my mind. It didn't really matter that I was over

Jana—when he saw that plan wasn't working, he'd just move on to another plan. Another more sophisticated and dangerous plan. He had been unstoppable only because I had never really tried to stop him.

I had to go on the offensive and either beat Terry at his own game or get taken down on the savannah.

The doorbell interrupted my thoughts, but before I could get to it, Mark had sprinted like he was on his way to a touchdown. My chances of pepperoni had just plummeted.

CHAPTER TEN

Pizza night had taken all of ten min-utes. My mom said we were a bunch of savages, but in my defense, if I didn't move fast Mark would inhale every scrap. Afterward, Rory staggered home in a cheesy haze and I jumped on the computer while my mom was on the phone with her friend Margie. Margie would keep my mom occupied for at least an hour, as she always had a lot to say about her no-good boss, a Miss Cheryl Crumstedder. Miss Crumstedder, if Margie were to be believed, was out to ruin Margie's life by insisting on knowing what Margie was doing all day long in her cubicle. Margie felt this was an outrageous invasion of privacy.

I'd made my decision. I was done being prey, it

was time to transform Chadwick Musselman into an apex predator.

I had gotten an idea on how to gaslight Terry Vance, and it would be the most epic revenge ever launched at Wayne Elementary. My first stop was Amazon and sure enough, there were fake bloody fingers for sale. There were also fake bloody ears and eyeballs, but I stayed focused. There were so many types of fake bloody fingers for sale that I started to wonder what other people were doing with them. I finally found a brand that really spoke to me. The fingers had a lot of fake blood on them and ragged edges that looked like skin hanging off. I bought eight packs of eight. Then I bought a Beast three-hundred-yard water balloon launcher. Then I bought a hammock chair. The fabric seat of the chair would be used to create a bigger pouch for the launcher. I spent my whole gift card from my birthday except for seventy-two cents. My arsenal would arrive in two days.

I surfed the internet to find the images I was looking for. It is really amazing that, whatever you need, somebody took the time to post it for you. I downloaded images of severed fingers and overturned

Jeeps and a crocodile with its jaws taped shut and ran them together in a video with *Jaws* music in the background.

I set up an Excel file and mapped out each step of the offensive. I had one week until the dance, and I would be ready.

Chadwick was cruising the savannah and ready to hunt.

* * *

At Suvi's house, I kicked Rory's leg to give him a sign. He was sprawled over a chair and would end up ruining the Singhs' furniture, just like he had at my house. I didn't know why I bothered, because he didn't get it. He stuffed his face with potato chips, wiped his hands on the arms of the chair, and said, "What?" As my dad has mentioned in the past, anthropologists should stop digging up old bones in search of the missing link because he's right here walking around the neighborhood.

Once the show started, I was hypnotized and

realized I would never be out of *Mission Almost Impossible*'s viselike grip. The finale would be three different challenges. Today, they were digging holes in the Mojave Desert. The first person to hit water would win that round. The show ended with Hank and Barb sunburned and coughing out sand, both up to their waists in holes in the desert.

After it was over, Suvi picked up a pair of glasses with thick black rims. They looked pretty scholarly. She put them on to read her notes on my psychoanalysis, but they must have been a strong prescription because she had to hold the paper really far away from her face.

"As we left our last session, you were going to reflect on who you really want to be," Dr. Singh said.

"I totally did," I said, more comfortable with talking in therapy this time. "I decided on apex predator."

Suvi scribbled furiously. I thought she seemed intrigued. "How do you propose to make the transition, Chadwick?" she asked.

"I'm going on the offensive. Defense never played to my strengths and it never worked. I'm going to launch the last prank that will be played between me and Terry, and it is going to be revenge on an epic scale. He got to play all the other ones, but I will have the last laugh. The last extremely long laugh."

Suvi took off her glasses. Her eyes refocused after she blinked a couple of times. "Interesting," she murmured.

"Yeah, so this is how it's going down," I said.

After I walked Suvi and Rory through my diabolical plan, Rory said, "That is the worst idea I ever heard!"

"Incorrect, Rory," Suvi said. "Chadwick's plan is brilliant. It will be a textbook demonstration of the reptilian brain overriding executive function."

I had no idea what Suvi was talking about, except for the part where she thought my plan was brilliant and that I might have a reptilian brain—who's the crocodile now?

"I'll need help," I said, "from both of you."

"I can't be involved," Rory said. "I'm already swamped. Susie Townsend said she might hang out at the dance with me."

"What does *might* mean?" Suvi asked.

"She said she reserved the right to accept better offers," Rory said. "Apparently, I always smell like Cheetos and it's gross. I'm okay with that complaint, because it takes the pressure off me. If she decides she *doesn't* want to hang out with me, I will automatically feel against her, so she goes right into my notebook. If she decides she *does* want to hang out with me and then I suddenly feel like I'm against it, I can just say she always smells like shampoo and it's gross and walk away. If she's not against it and I'm not against it, I'll eat a mint to cover up my Cheetos breath. Any way it goes, the power is in my hands."

I stared at Rory. It really was true that you couldn't help people until they were ready to help themselves. When Suvi was done psychoanalyzing me, I would slide over and make room on the couch for Rory.

"So you see what I mean?" Rory said. "I'll have a lot going on that night."

"You're my best friend," I said. "You have to help me. It's finally my moment to have my revenge and pull off an epic prank."

"Or," Rory muttered, "you could just give him back his stupid crayon."

"Remind me," I said, "if we were looking for Ring Dings, would we go to your house or mine?"

Rory moaned a little bit, like he was in the throes of a fever. "Ring Dings," he murmured. He was in.

Suvi said, "What do you need me to do?"

"Pose as my date," I said, "and bring a really big purse. That's how we'll get all the fingers inside the gym."

Suvi nodded. "I'll bring my beach bag, it's huge."

"Rory," I said, "I'll need your walkie-talkies. Bring them to the woods behind your house when you take the dog out for a walk tonight. Leave them by the old pine tree."

"What pine tree?" Rory said. "There's a thousand pine trees."

"The one that has candy bar wrappers littered all around it," I said.

"Oh, that pine tree," Rory said.

"I'll leave a bag of Cheetos there for you," I said, knowing full well that the lure of Cheetos in the woods would soothe Rory's resistance to my plan. He nodded and gazed over my head like he was daydreaming about Cheetos in the woods.

My troops were ready. I had one fierce lion and one best friend who, realistically, was more of a meerkat than an apex predator. It wasn't the army to end all armies, but it would have to be enough.

* * *

"You asked a girl!" my mom shrieked.

"I didn't ask a girl like how you think," I said. "It's just Suvi. She's only a friend."

"But Suvi is a girl, right?"

"Technically, she is," I said. "Anyway, I said we'd give her a ride because her parents are on call at the hospital."

"A girl!"

I had been afraid my mom was going to be that excited about me going to the dance with Suvi. It was almost like I had told her I was getting married. She planned a whole outing to the mall to get a new shirt and new sneakers, so there went my Saturday. Still, I felt like it wasn't so bad since volunteering to be a chaperone at the actual dance hadn't occurred to her. Also, my dad has privately told me and Mark that because we're a houseful of boys, sometimes we have to throw Mom a bone. I hadn't thrown one in a while, so bone officially thrown, Mom.

I didn't tell Mark about the epic revenge prank

because I was afraid he would have advice, mainly advice about how I shouldn't do it. I let him think that Suvi was my real date and he promised to tell me everything I would need to know about hanging out with a girl at a dance. Mark had been to five dances and danced with Cheryl at two of them. He said he had a lot of inside information that would help me look like I knew what I was doing. I felt myself go red at the mention of Cheryl, whose name I now associated with the inner sanctum break-in and brown eyes from Mars. I muttered, "Thanks, that would be great."

There were only six days left before the dance and I felt the time ticking away like minutes to liftoff. I realized that time went fast when you wanted it to go slow, and then it went slow when you wanted it to go fast. Up until then, I had never really understood the theory of relativity. But there you go—time is relative, and changes speed in exact relation to how you don't want it to. I would have to drop that knowledge into a conversation with my therapist. Suvi couldn't expect me to be as smart as she was, but it would be a nice surprise for her to find out that she had a patient who could sometimes talk to her on her own level.

The Amazon order arrived. I had raced home from the bus stop with Rory lagging behind. I didn't want Mark to see the box and start asking questions. When we got to my house, we didn't even open it; we took it over to Suvi's to test how it would all fit into the beach bag.

"Wow," Suvi said, unwrapping one of the fake fingers, "these look pretty real."

Suvi jumped up and pulled a medical book from a shelf and opened it to a page that showed various fingers and toes that had arrived at emergency departments separate from their owners.

"See what I mean?" she said.

I thought the pictures were interesting, but a little sickening. Rory turned greenish, but that's what happens when you eat a whole bowl of Fritos before you even have time to sit down.

The chair hammock I bought used carabiner clips to attach to holes in the wood frame of the hammock. I threw out the frame and clipped the carabiners around the rubber bands of the slingshot, creating a new supersized pouch. We went over the whole plan, step by step. Everybody knew what they were supposed to do and when they were supposed

to do it. Rory's walkie-talkies would keep us together like a coordinated strike force. Suvi packed it all in her beach bag, ready for action. The crocodile would take his last roll in the river.

*　*　*

Group remained determined to pry open the secrets of my brain. I was equally as determined to keep my private feelings where they belonged—buried deep in a vault called Do Not Open—Nobody Likes a Crybaby.

Mr. Samson rubbed his temples and said, "Here's the prompt question: What are you most frightened of? Well, let's see—I'm a thirty-five-year-old elementary school teacher with a receding hairline, crappy apartment, questionable clothes, and no girlfriend. All the dreams I had when I was young have been sucked into a vortex of mediocrity. What frightens me the most out of this whole nightmare? I guess that I will be lying on my deathbed and realize that one decision caused my whole crappy life. If you had just done this one thing, Bob Samson, everything would have been different. Like, if you had learned to play the guitar, you could have been a famous rock star with a supermodel girlfriend. But you didn't, and look what happened."

Mr. Samson was crumbling before our eyes.

Jana shared that she remained frightened that she wouldn't be thanked for all her dance committee efforts. She had stayed up late working on the dance budget. The herbed goat cheese on rice crisps that was supposed to lend class to the affair was too expensive, so she was going with Chex Mix instead.

"Chadwick? You're next," Mr. Samson said. "What keeps you up at night?"

I wasn't going to say what was really keeping me up at night—planning my revenge on Terry Vance. I wanted to lull Terry into a sense of security and make him believe I was the same old Chadwick. "I'm still being framed for crimes I didn't commit," I said.

"That's what you said last time. A total cop-out," Mr. Samson said. "Rory?"

"I'm afraid of pop quizzes. They put too much pressure on a person, and then the person goes totally blank, like their brain got put in a freezer, and then their math teacher says, 'Rory, it's like you're hearing about numbers for the first time.'"

"Cripes, really?" Mr. Samson said. "You two are pathetic. Terry?"

"Mr. Samson," Terry said, "I'm afraid I won't be able to do as much for my dad as I'd like to. I used to think we would go into business together and be the biggest mechanics in Pennsylvania, but that dream got crushed."

Mr. Samson held his face in his hands. He looked up and said, "That's what dreams are for, Terry. To get crushed."

The bell rang. Mr. Samson looked up at the ceiling and whispered, "Yes, God, you have just witnessed a snapshot of my life. Thanks for all your help."

After group, Jana shoved a piece of paper in my hand. I unfolded it. It was titled "OFFICIAL DANCE COMMITTEE NOTIFICATION." It said: "You are hereby informed that you are SO fired from the dance committee for committing voter fraud and bullying, which is SO disgusting. Regards, Chairman Sedgewick."

So that was that. I had thought that Jana would have noticed that I had stopped going to the meetings. I supposed she wanted to make sure I didn't suddenly reappear.

As she charged down the hall, I called after her, "Just because you have red hair and are popular doesn't mean everyone is in love with you. My therapist helped me see that."

It felt good to get that off my chest.

* * *

I had to have another meeting with Principal Grimeldi. She reviewed my new apology letter.

I'm sorry I got in trouble and got suspended. I hope I never get suspended again.
                                        Chadwick.

Principal Grimeldi sighed. "Just barely adequate."

Good enough!

"I tried to reach out to Dr. Silverstein," she continued, "to consult on your progress. I'm having trouble finding contact information for him. I Googled and found a dentist, but I cannot locate any listing at all for a children's therapist."

I wouldn't have thrown out Dr. Silverstein's name if I had known she would want to talk to him. If Principal Grimeldi talked to my dentist, all she'd find out was that I never floss and I'll pay for it later. "Oh . . ." I said, playing for time. "Well, Dr. Silverstein is very private and hates the internet and has an unlisted phone number and is retired."

"I see," Principal Grimeldi said, leaning back in her chair. "Then how did your parents find him?"

"Uh . . . he's my mom's cousin."

"Hm. Well, I would have liked to discuss my plans with him."

Plans? Why did she have plans for me? I already had my own plan—hand in my apology letter and disappear from view.

"Chadwick, you've come a long way, but it's critical for you to understand the effects of your actions. Once you have had the opportunity to stand in your victim's shoes, you will really internalize the consequences of bullying. Terry has graciously agreed to attend our session."

This couldn't be real. Vance was going to graciously come in and tell *me* what effect *my* actions had on *him*?

"Are you ready to face him, Chadwick?"

Principal Grimeldi peered at me like the answer to that question would tell her a lot. If I said no, I would probably be in these meetings for the rest of the year. "Uh, I guess," I said.

Terry walked in and sneered at me while Principal Grimeldi wasn't looking. I sneered back, but by then she was looking.

Principal Grimeldi frowned. "Not a very promising start, Chadwick." Then she instructed us that neither one of us was to speak in anger. She turned to Terry and said, "Why don't we begin by you telling Chadwick how his aggression made you feel."

Terry tried to look sad, but I knew he was taunting me. "Absolutely," he said. "I felt scared and have had trouble sleeping. I believe I may be psychologically scarred."

"Well said, Terry," Principal Grimeldi said. "Chadwick? How do you respond to Terry?"

Terry was psychologically scarred? My brains should have exploded out of my ears by now. Despite my plan to make Terry think I was the same old Chadwick, I couldn't resist. This was too much. "I'm not going along with this," I said. "That guy is the axis of evil. He's the Nile crocodile. He pretended he flunked and he framed me for voter fraud and he beat himself up on my locker and, trust me, he has no trouble sleeping." I turned to face Terry. "Well, I'm not putting up with it anymore, crocodile. You'll see. I'm turning the tables."

Terry flinched. He flinched just enough that I was sure he got my message. I was serious and he knew it.

He recovered himself and said, "Principal Grimeldi, now I am even more scarred."

Principal Grimeldi stood. "I'm disappointed in you, Chadwick. I'm so sorry, Terry. Clearly this is too soon." Then she muttered under her breath, "Exactly why I wanted to consult with the elusive Dr. Silverstein."

CHAPTER ELEVEN

Rory's mom had finally decided her elbow wasn't sore anymore and scheduled a tennis lesson. Mission Save Ourselves was ready to launch. Rory's dad paced the kitchen. He looked like he was about to faint. Mr. Richardson didn't handle pressure any better than Rory did.

"I'm off," Rory's mom called from the front hall. "There's seaweed crackers in the cabinet if you get hungry."

"Great!" Rory's dad said in a high, squeaky voice. "I love me some seaweed!"

I glanced at Rory. We would be lucky if we didn't have to call 911 and ask them to bring over some oxygen because Mr. Richardson was having a panic attack.

Rory's mom called, "Very funny." The front door banged shut.

Rory and I raced to the front windows and watched her car pull out of the driveway and head down the street.

"Is she gone?" Mr. Richardson asked, tiptoeing up behind us. "Totally gone?"

"Gone," I said. "She just turned the corner."

Mr. Richardson grabbed his car keys. "The mission is on!"

We unloaded the trunk of Mr. Richardson's car. I was pretty impressed with his selection. There were boxes and bags of Oreos, Doritos, Bugles, Twix, Chips Ahoy!, Cheetos, Ring Dings, Fritos, Funyuns, and Three Musketeers—a nice balance of salty and sweet.

We carried everything into the house. Rory and Mr. Richardson stood surveying their treasure, spread out on the hall floor.

"We'll never go hungry again, son."

Rory high-fived his dad. Then he said, "Wait a minute, where are the Cheetos? You got Cheetos, right?"

"I'd never forget the Cheetos," his dad said. "Cheetos are in the Richardson blood."

225

"They're probably still in the car," I said. "I'll go get them and shut the trunk."

I jogged out to the driveway and grabbed the family-sized bag of Cheetos. As I turned around, I noticed a car coming down the street. A car that looked suspiciously like Mrs. Richardson's. "Oh no," I said.

I slammed the trunk shut and ran into the house.

"She's coming back," I said, tossing the bag of Cheetos to Rory.

"Who? Who is coming back?" Mr. Richardson asked.

"Her," I said. "Mrs. Richardson."

"Her?" Mr. Richardson shrieked. "Why? Why would she come back?"

"She knows!" Rory said.

"Don't freak out," I said. "She probably just forgot something."

"No," Mr. Richardson said. "She never forgets anything. We do that." Mr. Richardson balled up his fists. "I knew that sore elbow was a ruse! How did she figure it out?"

"Save yourself!" Rory cried. He dropped the bag of Cheetos and ran out the back door. Mr. Richardson ran after him.

"No, you don't," I called after them. "You're not leaving me here to take the rap!" I ran out the back door after Rory and his dad.

I found them hiding in the woods behind the house. It was where Rory walked the dog to have a quiet snack before bed. He preferred sitting on the low branch of an old pine while the dog ran around, the giveaway being the candy wrappers everywhere. Apparently, Butterfingers were the new favorite. "How long are you going to stay here?" I asked.

Mr. Richardson paced between two spindly pines. "Until we dream up something plausible." He ran his hand through his hair. "Think! Why would Oreos and Cheetos suddenly appear in the house? Who brought them? A gift from a neighbor?"

"Yes!" Rory said. "And then we tried to give them back because we hate processed food but they said no, you have to take them," he added.

"That's good, Rory, keep talking," Mr. Richardson said.

"And then we were going to destroy it all and write a letter to the Cheetos company about how they're poisoning America," Rory said.

"That could work—your mom has written a couple of those letters herself."

"Well, I'm going home for lunch," I said. "Good luck!" As I walked home I noticed I was a little cheered up that somebody besides me had a problem. I knew it was wrong, but there it was.

* * *

That night, I waited until everybody went to bed and called Rory. "Are you still in the woods?"

"No," he whispered. "After an hour, we got cold. When we went inside the house, all our stuff was lined up on the kitchen counter and my mom was sitting at the table drumming her fingers. She said to my dad, 'I knew something was up. You've never built anything in your entire life. I found the secret cabinet in the basement, which I assume was part of the plan to ruin your health.' It was every man for himself, so I told her I had fallen under my dad's bad influence."

"Did she buy that?" I asked.

"Yup. I think he's grounded."

"I guess it could have been worse."

"Not really," Rory said. "After my mom gave us a lecture about junk food, my dad cracked under the pressure and confessed to leaving me candy bars in the back seat of the car, so that routine is totally shut down. It's not even safe to bring home the baggies of snacks I get from your house—I used to bring some of it into the house. Like if I took ham or cheese, I'd hide it in the very back of the refrigerator. Now I'll have to leave everything in the woods. I'm going to buy mints and keep them with me so I'm always prepared in case she wants to check my breath for Cheetos. She said she's going to be watching us like a hawk."

* * *

It was finally the night of the dance and I was jittery with the anticipation of my bloody-fingers prank. I was doing my best to act normal in front of my mom, but her X-ray vision saw right through my act. Fortunately, she assumed I was nervous because I had asked a girl to hang out with me. She kept saying things like, "Remember, honey, girls are people too."

I had already been standing on the stairs for ten minutes while my mom went back and forth getting close-ups and long shots and trying to make me pose so we could have memories forever.

For the hour before I'd even made it to the stairs, Mark had paced my room, giving me advice on how to act at a dance. Some of what he said sounded right, like offer to get the girl some punch and don't stand in a corner with a bunch of guys pretending you don't know her. Other advice seemed wrong, like his demonstration on how to slow dance. It felt like we were two old people shuffling around a home for the aged. I had to go along with it since I couldn't exactly tell him that I was not going to be dancing. I would be too busy being epic to have time to dance.

My mom made me sit on the stairs and prop my chin on my hands. I would have to get ahold of her phone and delete all of the embarrassing evidence later.

"You can't take pictures at Suvi's house," I said. It was already on the list I'd given my mom that morning. It was a whole page of detailed instructions on what not to do or say in front of Suvi, but I wasn't sure she had really read it. She had barely glanced at it and thrown it into her purse. Now I was thinking of even more things to add.

I finally lured her away from the stairs and out to the car. Before we could get out of the driveway, Mark ran out and banged on my window. I put it down and he said, "And don't be the last one to leave. Very uncool."

I suppose he should have directed that to our mom, since I wasn't actually driving. "Thanks," I said. "I won't."

He stood at the end of the driveway and waved us off until we finally turned a corner.

"Did you use deodorant soap?" my mom asked, driving at her usual careful speed. "Not the Ivory soap—that won't control odor at all."

"Uh, I think so," I said.

"Well, if you didn't, I guess there's nothing we can do about it now," she said.

I lifted my arm and smelled. I couldn't tell.

For the rest of the ride, my mom took herself on a walk down memory lane. The first time she'd danced with my dad she'd had to make a serious decision about whether she could have a relationship with a man who couldn't dance. What she should have really considered was whether she could deal with a man who would *never* learn how to dance. He had sworn he would take lessons before their wedding, but based on the bruises on her feet after the bride-and-groom dance, he hadn't. She only hoped, for my sake, it wasn't genetic.

We finally rolled to a stop in front of Suvi's house. I tried to get my mom to stay in the car. I told her I was pretty sure that only Suvi would be there, as the Doctors Singh spent their whole lives in surgery, sewing up the injured. She swung her door open and said, "Don't be ridiculous, I can't wait to meet her parents."

I could only hope she didn't ask the doctors if they had used deodorant soap. With any luck, they really were in surgery.

We had barely knocked on the door when it swung open.

Mrs. Dr. Singh was tall, like Suvi. She and my mom looked at each other and then they started talking rapid-fire. I'd seen this before with my mom. When we were in the grocery store, if she saw another lady looking at the same product, they could talk about it for twenty minutes. I was pretty sure that area mothers communicated using a secret Facebook group so when they finally ran into each other it was like they were best friends already.

"My husband got called in for an emergency surgery," Dr. Singh said, "so I promised him lots of pictures."

Pictures? Of the both of us? Together? Did Suvi forget to give her mom a list of dos and don'ts?

"Well, look at you," Dr. Singh said to me. "You look very smart in that outfit."

"Chadwick has been so excited about the dance," my mom said.

I never said that! Do not invent things you wish I said!

"That is such an interesting name," Dr. Singh said. "I don't think I've ever met a Chadwick before."

"Oh, I'll tell you the story behind it," my mom said.

Don't tell that story! It's on the list! Right at the top!

"My husband wanted to name him after his grandfather, Wick. I wanted to name him after my father, Chad. We argued about it for a whole day while our nameless baby boy lay in a bassinet. That night, my husband showed up with a bunch of tulips and said, 'How about we name him Chadwick?'"

Dr. Singh was smiling at my mom, but I knew what she was thinking—one bunch of tulips saddled that kid with the name Chadwick?

Suvi appeared at the top of the stairs. She looked pretty magnificent. She wore a blue dress with a silver belt and her hair was up in a ponytail. It kind of gave me a queasy feeling. I knew we were going on a mission, not a date, but it looked so much like we were going to the dance together that it was a little nerve-racking.

Then I noticed the beach bag over her shoulder. It was massive. Even I could see that it didn't look right with her outfit.

"There she is!" Dr. Singh said. "Now you two, stand on the stairs together and we'll get some pictures."

I had not factored in the whole parent moment when I had laid out my plan. I trudged up the stairs while Suvi trudged down the stairs. We met halfway and looked past each other. Then I went up an extra step to try to even out our heights.

"Suvi, honey," her mom said, "I'm sure you don't

need a bag that big. It looks like you've packed for a weekend."

"I have a lot of stuff," Suvi said in a really impressive preteen "question me further at your peril" voice.

"Kids," Dr. Singh said to my mom, shaking her head and laughing.

As my mom and Dr. Singh got out their phones, Suvi whispered, "Bloody fingers, giant slingshot, and walkie-talkie are a go."

"Video is a go," I whispered back, patting the flash drive in my pocket. "Rory has the other walkie-talkie."

"Okay, smile," Dr. Singh called.

"This is too cute!" my mom said.

"Parents," Suvi muttered. "Unbelievable."

"Totally unbelievable," I said, the mutual disdain for our parents driving some of the queasiness out of my stomach.

"My baby's first dance," Dr. Singh said.

My mom leaned over to Dr. Singh and said, "They look so grown-up!"

"I know," Dr. Singh said. "It seems like only yesterday they were drooling in their high chairs."

"Tell me about it," my mom said, "if there's one thing I don't miss about babies, it's the cleanup. You get one end cleaned just in time to start cleaning the other end."

Maybe I should have recruited my mom into my army. She's one of the most frightening people I know.

We finally got out of the house. Dr. Singh stood at the door, watching us head to the car. She waved and then snapped a few photos of us getting inside. I sank in my seat as my mom waved back at her out the car window. Then they kept waving like one of them was boarding a ship for an ocean crossing and it would be many years before they saw each other again.

Moments after we pulled away, I had a revelation. Trying to imagine how a particular scenario will play out is pointless, because no matter how much you think about it you can't factor in everything. I had prepared a whole review of the steps of the prank for Suvi, but I'd totally forgotten about the pair of ears attached to the individual driving the car.

I tried to think of something else to talk about. I couldn't use any of my *Mission Almost Impossible* conversations because I wasn't supposed to be watching it. I couldn't use the recent "unbelievable parents" conversation, because one of the unbelievable parents was in the car.

The queasy feeling started to come back. My mom was probably wondering why I wasn't talking to my date. How could I be so nervous? It wasn't a real date, it just looked like one. Then it occurred to me that if just looking like a date made me feel sick, how I would stop myself from projectile vomiting on a real one?

I searched my mind for any topic, any topic at all. Finally, I said, "Rory still doesn't know if Susie Townsend is going to hang out with him at the dance. She's waiting until the very last minute for other offers."

"How's he supposed to know what she decided?" Suvi asked.

"She'll find him at the dance and wink. The right eye means yes and the left eye means no. If she says yes, he'll decide if he can handle it. So they'll either be hanging out, or else he'll tell Susie she smells like shampoo and walk away."

"Oh."

And . . . hello, silence.

I willed my mom to go faster. *Stop hitting the brakes every time you see a yellow light! A yellow light means caution, so just cautiously keep going! My nerves are cracking under the pressure of your slowness!*

"Suvi," my mom said, "Chadwick hasn't told me a thing. How did he ask you to the dance? How long have you two been an item?"

Did she just say that out loud? An item? I didn't dare look at Suvi. I stared straight ahead and tried to burn the back of my mom's head with a death stare.

"Well . . ." Suvi said, playing for time, "I can't remember exactly what he said."

"You look cute together," my mom said.

Apparently, Mrs. Musselman was immune to the effects of my death stare.

"And just wait until next year," she went on, like she was a kamikaze pilot determined to destroy the enemy target with a hail of embarrassment gunfire, "his brother shot up like a rocket in seventh grade."

"Oh," Suvi said, "I guess that's something to look forward to."

Now I really couldn't talk. I couldn't think of anything to say, and even if I did there was the danger that my mom might decide to join the conversation. Before I knew it, we'd be talking about how I only stopped wetting the bed because I wanted to go to kindergarten.

Finally, we got to the school. My mom reminded us she would be back at ten o'clock. Three times. I had to point out that she was starting to hold up a line of cars before she agreed to pull away. She was crying when she left. My mom gets emotional about what she calls the magical moments of childhood, so

I supposed she thought this was one of them. I wondered what she would think if she knew I was practically sick in the car from just seeming like I was on a date and having to live through all her "you look cute together" talk.

CHAPTER TWELVE

The gym had been transformed. Lights were strung on plastic blow-up palm trees and somebody had painted a mural of the sun setting over a beach that looked like an actual sunset. Four television screens were set up, one on each wall. Toward the far side of the gym, two long tables were covered in white tablecloths. One had bowls of Chex Mix lined up from end to end and the other had buckets with bottles of water floating in melting ice.

Somehow, I had not thought it would look so officially like a dance. It was the first one I had ever been to. I could have gone to the one last year, but Rory and I had decided that it sounded stupid, stayed at my house, and watched a movie. At least, that's why we said we didn't want to go. Privately, I had looked upon the whole thing as a fright-night sort of experience. There were just too many unknowns and I had never asked a girl to dance. At that point, I had never really asked a girl anything. At that point, I had not even noticed Jana.

Things had really changed since then. I'd spent the past summer lurking my way into Jana's overlap group, gotten to know her, and then realized I didn't like her as much as I thought. Or at all, really. Now I was at a dance with Suvi, who just months ago I would have sworn I would never willingly talk to because of her extreme smartness.

I looked at Suvi surveying the crowd with her huge beach bag over her arm. She really did look great. If I were on a real date with somebody like her I'd probably have to excuse myself and go hyperventilate in the bathroom.

Suvi said, "Objective number one, exit via the boys' locker room and ensure our asset on the outside is in position. Return to the girls' locker room door. I'll have it propped open. Then we launch the communication."

"Wait," I said, "what's the asset?"

"Rory."

"Oh," I said, beginning to understand Suvi's military lingo. "And the communication is the phone call?"

"Roger," she said.

"Who's Roger?" I asked.

"It means yes."

"Got it," I said. I probably should have looked up this stuff ahead of time. I should have known that Suvi would be überprepared. She had probably interviewed a member of the military while Rory and I were lounging around eating Ring Dings.

Suvi headed toward the girls' locker room and I ran through the boys'. The door said "Exit Only" but it didn't have an alarm on it. I flew out to the back of the school.

I ran around the building and along the trees that lined the drive leading to the front of the gym. "Rory!" I called. "Rory!"

"I'm over here," I heard from a clump of bushes next to an old oak tree that had a good view of the drive.

I jogged over to the sound of his voice. Rory switched on a flashlight. He sat on the grass, surrounded by snack-sized bags of Cheetos and a pile of empty Butter-finger wrappers.

He saw me staring at them and said, "I didn't know how long I would be stuck out here. I told my dad we were all supposed to bring something to the dance and he swung by the Wawa. He's been avoiding convenience stores ever since Mission Save Ourselves went down in flames. He says it's better to just avoid the temptation. I think he's right—he lost his mind in there and now he's driving around eating a family-sized bag of Funyuns. Anyway, I have plenty—you want some?"

"No," I said, "I'm too nervous to eat."

"Really? That has never, ever happened to me."

"You have your walkie-talkie?"

Rory rummaged around his bags. "Here it is," he said, holding it up.

"Good. Now, when you see Mr. Vance's van, radio in to us—the eagle has landed."

"I got it," Rory said. "You've made me practice it a hundred times. I see the van with 'Vance Auto Repair' on the side, I hit talk and say the eagle has landed."

"Great," I said. "I think we're ready."

"I hope so," Rory said. "Susie Townsend is probably looking for me. I can't stay out here all night."

"Oh," I said, surprised, "so you decided to hang out with her?"

"I think so," Rory said, shoving a handful of Cheetos in his mouth. "I'll know definitely when I see her."

"Did you bring breath mints?" I asked.

"No!" Rory cried, slapping his forehead and leaving a trail of orange crumbs on it. "Why do I always forget something! What am I going to do?"

"I'll find you some later," I said, "just stay focused."

I ran to the back of the gym and found the door to the girls' locker room propped open. I slipped in and looked around in the dim light. I had never been in the girls' locker room before. It was the exact same setup as the boys', except it didn't smell the same. It smelled cleaner. Like not so many socks had been in it.

I found Suvi lurking in the shadows. "Our asset is in place," I whispered. "Launch the communication."

Suvi nodded and pulled out her phone. The day before, we had logged on to her carrier and changed her name to Principal so it would come up as that name on Mr. Vance's phone. She speed-dialed Mr. Vance.

We stood there in the darkness. It was so quiet I could hear it ring. Then a gruff voice. "Hello?"

Suvi took a deep breath. "Mr. Vance? So sorry to trouble you. This is Pamela Grimeldi, your son's principal at Wayne Elementary."

"Whatever it is, I'll have to see proof," Mr. Vance said.

"Oh no, Mr. Vance, Terry is not in trouble," Suvi said. "I am calling to inform you that we believe Terry is having some sort of allergic reaction. The nurse is with him now, as she was helping us chaperone the dance, but we fear we may have to call an ambulance. Would you please come down?"

"What did he eat?" Mr. Vance asked. "He's never been allergic to anything. The kid ate an oil filter a couple years back and he was fine."

"Um," Suvi said, "I can't be sure about the particular culprit. There appear to be some unusual ingredients in the Chex Mix."

I covered my mouth to hold back a snort of laughter.

Mr. Vance said, "Crap. On my way," and hung up the phone.

I leaned against the lockers. It was all happening. We were doing it.

Suvi dug through her beach bag, pulled out a walkie-talkie, and handed it to me. I held it up and pressed talk. "The eagle has taken flight. I repeat, the eagle has taken flight."

I took my finger off the talk button for the answer. I heard crunching, then a mumbled, "Got it."

"Let's get the slingshot in place," I said. We had decided to use a leg on either end of the table that held Jana's Chex Mix to anchor the rubber bands.

The tablecloth would hide it for us and it was the perfect angle to aim for the center of the gym. We'd tuck the slingshot underneath until we were ready, then grab it, dump the bloody fingers into the pouch, pull it back, and fire.

We slipped out of the locker room and headed toward the tables. We got behind them and Suvi dropped her beach bag, but just then Principal Grimeldi appeared. "I had quite forgotten you two were on the dance committee," she said. She looked over the tables. "Everything seems in good order, no need to work all night."

Suvi pushed the beach bag underneath the table with her foot.

"Go ahead now," the principal said, smiling.

"Go where?" I asked, my teeth chattering as I spoke.

"Out there, to the dance floor," she said.

I noticed droplets of sweat running down the sides of my shirt. Principal Grimeldi had nearly caught us and now Suvi was leading me to the dance floor. Dancing had not been in the plan! Dancing to a Bruno Mars song with a lot of random changes in beats was really not in the plan!

I remembered seeing the music video and did my best to do what Bruno did. I snapped my fingers over my head and swiveled my hips. At least, I hoped it was a swivel. I swung my arms around. Suvi leapt out of the way and almost fell down. Somehow my arms had transformed into lethal weapons, and I'd come pretty close to hitting her in the face. I put them straight down against my sides where they couldn't kill anybody. My feet were doing their best to keep up with Bruno Mars, but he seemed to be always one step ahead of me. Suvi looked at me like I was having some kind of seizure. I wasn't that surprised, since it *felt* like I was having some kind of seizure.

I did a twirl so I could see where Principal Grimeldi was. She had moved away from the table and had made her way up to the stage. I turned to Suvi and snapped my fingers while pointing to the table to signal that the coast was clear.

The nominees for queen and king were heading up to the stage. Principal Grimeldi held a silver platter with the crowns on it. The music suddenly shut off and she turned on the microphone. "Good evening, everybody. We have come to the moment where we crown our queen and our king."

Suvi and I had backed off the dance floor and into the relative darkness next to the snack table. Nobody was looking at us; they were too busy admiring the nominees for queen and king of the dance.

Principal Grimeldi unfolded one of the cards in her hand and said, "This year's queen is Jana Sedgewick!"

The crowd clapped. Suvi rolled her eyes and said, "Really? I voted for Tomiko. Who did you vote for?"

"Um . . . I'm pretty sure Tomiko too," I said.

Jana proudly wore her crown while the other nominees for queen shuffled off the stage. Somebody in the crowd shouted, "Robbed!" I assumed it was Bethany.

"And our king of the dance is Terry Vance!" Principal Grimeldi said from the stage.

The crowd clapped as the crown was placed on Terry's head. He smiled and led Jana out onto the floor for the queen and king dance.

"I can't believe he is king of the dance. Look at him—he thinks he's won. Wait until everybody finds out they voted for a fraud," I whispered as we sidled in front of the slingshot at our feet.

"Stay on the mission," Suvi said, looking as determined as a lion tracking a wounded gazelle.

"Right," I said.

Suvi and I slowly sank down until we were on our knees. Suvi pulled the slingshot out of her beach bag and I lifted up the leg of the table, which was way heavier than I thought it would be, and put the leg inside the loop of rubber. Suvi did the same on her end. We pushed the pouch underneath so it was hidden by the tablecloth. Slingshot in place.

"The video is next," Suvi said.

"Right."

I knew from dance-committee meetings that the screens set up all over the gym would be hooked up to wifi, ready to play hula music from YouTube when it was time for the hula dance off. All I had to do was plug in my drive to the main monitor and grab the remote control. When we were ready, I'd switch the input.

One of the screens was bigger than the others. I motioned to Suvi and we turned our backs on the dancers. Sure enough, there was a remote control sitting on the bleachers right next to it.

I grabbed the flash drive from my pocket and plugged it into the monitor.

Suvi high-fived me. Everything was in place. All we were waiting for was Rory's signal that Mr. Vance was on his way up the drive.

I waited impatiently. It would be perfect timing if Mr. Vance would show up now—while the crocodile was dancing with his queen. Fortunately, they were dancing to the school song, a dreary slow song that went on forever about school spirit and honor and hard work and I didn't know what else.

I could just see Jana's red hair bobbing over the heads of the onlookers. It looked like a fireball under the spotlights.

My walkie-talkie sprang to life and crackled. "The eagle has landed," Rory said. "Can I come in now?"

"Roger that," I said.

"It's Rory," Rory radioed back. "Who's Roger?"

"Nobody," I answered. "Just come on in." I turned to Suvi. "This is it."

We bent down, grabbed the slingshot, and stared at the door.

The minutes seemed to tick on forever. Where was Mr. Vance? The school song was coming to an end.

"There he is," Suvi said.

Mr. Vance had just pushed open the double doors.

I hit the input on the remote control. Suvi dumped the fake fingers out of her beach bag and into the giant pouch while I held it open. We grabbed the pouch on either side and ran backward to stretch the rubber bands as far as we could.

"One, two, three, FIRE!" I shouted.

The school song was drowned out by the *Jaws* music. Jeeps and bloody fingers spun on the video screens. Sixty-four fake fingers launched out of the slingshot and peppered the dancers.

It was the most magical moment of my life.

With one shot, Chadwick Musselman had pulled off an epic revenge.

CHAPTER THIRTEEN

Girls screamed. In the dim light of the gym, the bloody fingers flying everywhere looked totally real. Marilee Marksley pulled one out of her hair. Carmen Rodriguez brushed one off her shoulder like it was a live spider. One had landed perfectly and sat upright on Terry's crown.

Principal Grimeldi stood on the stage calling for order and shouting for somebody to turn off the video. I put the remote control in Jana's Chex Mix and swaggered into the chaos.

Mr. Vance kicked some fingers out of the way and marched toward his son. He tapped Terry on the shoulder just as my video came to its amazing conclusion—a picture of a crocodile with its jaws duct-taped shut.

The sudden end of the video made the silence deafening.

"Well," Mr. Vance said to his son, "you look fine to me."

"What?" Terry said. "Why are you here?" he asked his dad.

"Because your principal said you were having an allergic attack and she was thinking about calling an ambulance."

All eyes turned to Principal Grimeldi. She said, "I certainly did not make such a call, Mr. Vance."

Mr. Vance eyed Ms. Grimeldi. He picked the fake finger from the top of Terry's crown. "What kind of operation are you running here anyway?"

"I can assure you I don't know what has happened," the principal said, "but this is certainly *not* part of the evening's programming."

"Mr. Vance?" I said, loudly. "Mr. Vance! It's a miracle! You grew back all your fingers!"

Mr. Vance looked at me like I was nuts.

The chattering began immediately.

"He does have all his fingers."

"Didn't Terry say his dad lost eight of them in a Jeep accident?"

"How could he get them back?"

"I bet he never lost them in the first place!"

"I can see his fingers," Marilee Marksley shouted, "with My Own Eyes."

I watched Terry's face. First he looked confused. Then he looked at the video of the duct-taped crocodile. Then he looked at the fake bloody fingers at his feet.

Then he looked at me. He knew I had done it. He knew I had meant it when I'd said the tables had turned. I had finally gotten my revenge.

Then I noticed that he wasn't looking at me like he had looked the last time I'd played a prank on him. That time, when I'd pulled out his chair, I'd worried that I might find him standing over my bed with a hatchet in the middle of the night. This time I started to wonder if I would wake up in the middle of the night and find him standing over me with an already-bloody hatchet and my legs and arms located elsewhere in the room.

I briefly considered diving under the Chex Mix table.

But no, this was my moment. I had won.

"Mr. Vance," Principal Grimeldi said, "I am sure there is some explanation for this—"

"Never mind," Mr. Vance said. "The kid seems fine, I'm going home. Carry on with whatever kind of crackpot show you're running. I'm always glad to see my tax dollars at work."

Mr. Vance strode out of the gym, seemingly unaware that he had just played a part in his offspring's utter takedown.

Jana said, "I don't get it. That was your dad? Why does he have all his fingers?"

Terry seemed to be searching his mind for some explanation. I decided to explain it for him. "Terry lied about the whole tragic story," I said. "Terry Vance? Not tragic."

Jana stared at Terry. Then she said, "That is just disgusting," and stomped away.

I crossed my arms. "Well," I said, "it looks like you're about to be a loner again."

"Or," Terry said, "it looks like you're about to be suspended again."

I ignored that threat. I'd already been suspended once and it wasn't that bad. "Everybody knows you lied," I said. "There's nothing interesting about you; you had to make it all up to get Jana to like you."

Terry took a sharp intake of breath. I had hit home on that one. He knew he would have never been a part of Jana's clique if he hadn't pretended to be tragic.

And now he had been humiliated in front of the whole school and he knew that I had done it. I was finally vindicated.

I waited for the surge of confidence, the swagger of the apex predator.

I stared at Terry, daring him to say something.

His eye twitched and he turned away.

My victory congratulations came to a halt. Terry's eye had twitched. Just like it had twitched when I took the crayon in first grade. On that day, I had wondered if he would cry. Was he going to cry now? He was supposed to be mad but admitting defeat, not twitching. We were supposed to be two worthy opponents, going mano a mano, with me claiming victory and him waving a white flag in defeat. This was just sad.

A sick feeling began to crawl all over me.

"Geez, Chadwick," Rory said, coming up behind

me, "why couldn't you just give him back his stupid crayon?"

Why couldn't I? Why didn't I? How did I ever think this was a good idea? Suvi had thought it was a good idea. Could I blame it on her? Could I blame Dr. Singh? Anybody?

No, it was all on me. I'd thought up the epic revenge. I'd bought the fake bloody fingers and the slingshot. I'd made the video. I'd recruited my army of two. I had humiliated him in front of the whole school. I had been successful, only now I was starting to think that what I had really done was turn myself into . . . Terry Vance.

I was him. I was everything I didn't like about the Nile crocodile. I had executed an apex predator ambush. It had seemed like such a good idea at the time, but now it didn't feel like such a good idea.

"Oh no," I whispered.

Terry wasn't looking at me anymore. He was looking at Jana, who was now surrounded by Carmen and Bethany. They were picking out the good parts of the Chex Mix to try to cheer her up.

He liked her. I could see that he actually liked her.

He had been trying to drive me crazy by turning Jana against me, but instead I had ended up driving him crazy by turning Jana against him. It should be justice, like Suvi said, an eye for an eye. It didn't feel like justice, though.

This wasn't first grade. I couldn't just forgive myself and then blame my teacher. I had to fix it.

I grabbed Suvi's arm. "Don't let Terry go anywhere," I said. "I'll be back as soon as I can!"

"There's more?" Suvi asked with real enthusiasm.

I didn't answer. I raced to the back of the gym. With any luck, the door that led into the school would be unlocked. I grabbed the handle.

Yes! I was in.

I ran down the hall toward the art room. I threw on the lights and jogged toward the shelves that had the markers and colored pencils and chalk . . . and crayons.

I dumped a box of sixty-four on the floor and got down on my knees, searching for the sunset orange.

I grabbed it and stood up victorious. This madness had to end. I would finally give Terry Vance his crayon back. Then, I would figure out what to do about the rest of the school. Maybe say that Mr. Vance was Terry's uncle and that I had seen his fingerless dad with My Own Eyes? It worked for Marilee, so why not me? Whatever I would become on the savannah of Wayne Elementary, it was *not* going to be a crocodile.

* * *

When I got back to the gym, the music was on again, but Principal Grimeldi was looking at the main monitor and talking to one of the other chaperones. She pointed at the flash drive and then took it and put it in her pocket. It would only be a matter of time before I was busted.

Where was Terry?

Rory stood next to Susie Townsend, who appeared to be leaning away from him. I guessed he hadn't found any breath mints.

I ran over to Suvi. "Where is he?" I asked. "I got the crayon."

Suvi said, "He left. I told him you wanted him to stay, but he left anyway. What are we going to do with a crayon? I don't remember that being in the plan."

Was I too late? No, I couldn't be. I had to find him. "Suvi," I said, "I'm going to ask you to put on your Dr. Singh hat for a moment. No more revenge plots—I'm going to apologize to Terry like I should have done in first grade."

Suvi nodded and said, "That is very mature, Chadwick. Though Suvi still stands by an eye for an eye."

I left Suvi and Dr. Singh and ran out the doors of the school. In the distance, I saw Terry striding down the drive.

"Terry," I shouted. "Terry, wait!"

I ran after him as fast as I could.

"Terry," I said, grabbing his sleeve.

Terry Vance stopped and turned to look at me. "What do you want now?" he said.

"I want to apologize," I said. "I shouldn't have done that. It was really stupid. *I* was really stupid. I'll stick up for you. I'll tell everybody that was your uncle, not your dad. That way, you can go on having a fingerless dad and Jana will still like you."

Terry stared at me, expressionless.

I slowly held out my hand and unfolded my palm. The sunset-orange crayon lay there, lighted by the moon.

"I came to give you back your crayon," I said solemnly. "You had every right to color with it. I should have never taken it from you."

Terry stared down at the crayon.

"It's finally over," I said. "You won. I gave you back the crayon I took all those years ago. We can finally stop all this."

Terry took the crayon from my palm. He examined it, rolling it between his fingers.

Then he snapped it in half.

I stared at the pieces of crayon, the ragged edges of the paper hanging off the broken ends of wax.

Terry leaned close to me and whispered in my ear. "Here's the thing, Musselman—you could have apologized that day, or the next day, or even the next year. But you didn't, and now you've just raised the stakes, my friend. I've been dogging you for so long that it's turned into a hobby, but now I'm going to make it a full-time career. I've got three notebooks full of plans to go home and look at."

The crocodile smiled at me and flung the two pieces of sunset-orange crayon over his shoulder.

Terry Vance had three notebooks full of plans. It had been a hobby; now it was going to be his career. Full-time.

I would go forward into the future knowing that the crocodile would always be lurking on the riverbank, biding his time and waiting to strike.

No, I wouldn't let that happen. I might not want to be a crocodile, but I wasn't going back to being a helpless flamingo either. "Oh, yeah," I said, "well, how do you know I don't have my own notebooks full of plans?"

"Who cares?" Terry asked. "They'll never be as good as my plans. I've even got one where you get arrested for robbing a bank. That one's not until high school, though."

Robbing a bank. And it was scheduled? There was an actual schedule?

I clasped my hands in front of me so it wouldn't be noticeable that they were shaking. "That's nothing," I said. "I have one where you think Tom Brady from the Patriots is following you on Instagram, but it's really me."

I was pretty impressed with myself for coming up with that on the fly.

Terry snorted. "You kinda gave that one away, I'll keep an eye out for it. That is, if I have time while I'm busy cutting the brake lines on your bike."

I noticed I had a hard time swallowing the saliva in my mouth. "When is that scheduled for?" I croaked out.

"It's a surprise," Terry said.

My mind was racing in two different directions—one, imagining riding my bike down Chancery Hill only to discover I had no brakes and was plummeting to my death, and two, what to say next.

"Tampering with a bike," I said in as dismissive a tone as I could muster, "is so unoriginal. Especially because I plan to set off fireworks. Inside your house."

"Are you sure you won't run into any booby traps that might guillotine you before you got inside?" Terry asked. "I'd hate to see your head rolling down the driveway because of a careless accident."

"We're both going to end up dead, aren't we?" I whispered.

"Probably."

"I don't want to die," I said. "Do you?"

"No," Terry said, "but I will if I have to."

And there it was. The most important thing to know about Terry Vance: He would die if he had to.

"Maybe we don't have to die," I said, trying to keep the sound of desperation out of my voice. "Maybe we could negotiate some kind of settlement."

"What's in it for me?" Terry asked.

What was in it for Terry? What weapon did I have against the Nile crocodile? What did I have over the guy who had me scheduled to rob a bank?

The answer hit me like a bolt of lightning.

"Well," I said, "it's not just me you're up against now. Suvi is pretty enthusiastic about what she calls an eye for an eye. I've actually had to rein her in on a couple of her ideas. She's as unpredictable as a wolverine."

"She's just a girl," Terry said, but I thought I heard the smallest amount of hesitation in his voice.

"She's just a girl," I answered, "whose first idea was to break into a morgue and get real fingers to launch."

Suvi hadn't suggested that, but if she had I wouldn't have been that surprised.

Terry considered the matter of Suvi Singh breaking into the morgue.

"And," I went on, "when she talks about an eye for an eye, I think she might mean actual eyes."

Terry chewed on his lip as he mulled over Suvi coming for one of his eyes.

"Her parents are doctors," I said. "They probably have scalpels lying all over the house."

Terry rubbed at one of his eyes like Suvi was already on her way to get it. Terry Vance might not be afraid to die, but it appeared that he *was* afraid of being maimed.

"For all I know," I said, "she already has a whole collection of eyes from people who have crossed her."

Terry slowly blinked as if he was checking that both of his eyes were still there.

He folded his arms and said, "If I'm going to give up making your life miserable, I'll need a lawyer to negotiate the terms. And confirm that I won't lose any eyes."

CHAPTER FOURTEEN

After Terry and I worked out the where and when to negotiate a settlement, I went back into the gym and turned myself in. I figured why spend days looking over my shoulder when I already knew I would get caught? This way, I could just get it over with. I claimed I had worked alone, a rogue prankster, so Suvi and Rory wouldn't get in trouble. Naturally, my mom and dad were disappointed in me. (Though my dad seemed way less disappointed than my mom and kept asking for more and more details.) I was suspended for another week, but I had become an old hand at suspension so I just grabbed a plate of bacon and kicked back with the Reality 24/7 network.

Now I was back. Marilee stood on the bleachers and silence descended on the crowd. There had been so much gossip swirling around the school that the briefings were now held daily. I had edged in closer than I usually would because I knew I would be one of the subjects. Rory had told me that I had been in the briefing every single day while I was out. Apparently, there had been talk that some of the bloody fingers had been real and the police were trying to locate citizens with missing fingers. I supposed Terry had told somebody that Suvi had considered getting them from the morgue and the rumor mill had taken it from there.

"I saw, with My Own Eyes," Marilee said in a grave voice, "what our own Terry Vance is creating. I do not exaggerate when I say it's a masterpiece."

I looked at Rory. Masterpiece? What masterpiece? Rory shrugged.

"Terry is a gifted novelist," Marilee said. "Perhaps one of the greatest of our time. Like many artists before him, he is brooding and troubled. He even, at times, has difficulty removing himself from the compelling fictional world he is creating. That was how he began to believe that his own father had lost all his fingers—because the hero in his novel lost all his fingers in a tragic Jeep accident."

The crowd began to chatter. "Oh, so his dad never lost his fingers, Terry just thought he did." "I heard artists have to be a little crazy to create a masterpiece, he must be *really* good."

"Gifted novelist?" I whispered. "Where did that come from?"

"So wait a minute," Jana said, "Terry wasn't lying, he was just lost in a fictional world because he's an artistic genius?"

"Precisely," Marilee said.

Jana stood up and gazed around the school yard. "I've totally wronged him," she said softly.

"What is going on?" I whispered to Rory. "Now Terry Vance is a tortured but talented novelist? Are you kidding me?"

"Further," Marilee said, "the settlement negotiations between Terry and Chadwick are scheduled to commence on Thursday, after school. I will be following that story closely and you will be the first to know any breaking news on that front."

Great. I had thought I would start the settlement negotiations from a power position. Now it looked like not only would Terry be forgiven for lying, but he was going to get credit for it. It wasn't enough that he was a likable vampire, now he was a brooding novelist too.

Terry Vance, the guy who had only gone into the library one time in his whole life, to check out a book about gaslighting, was now a novelist. There was no way that Marilee believed it. She hadn't seen any kind of literary masterpiece with Her Own Eyes. But I thought I knew how she had been inspired to say that she had.

The crowd dispersed and I climbed the bleachers to Marilee. I leaned close to her ear and said, "How many Snickers bars did Terry give you to float that ridiculous story?"

Marilee smiled and said softly, "Quite a few, Chadwick. Quite a few."

* * *

Representation for the parties in the settlement negotiations between me and Terry had been finalized. I had Rory and Suvi on my side of the table. Mark had been ruled out because he was too big and didn't go to our school and would be intimidating to the other side. Suvi was almost ruled out because she was too smart, but that would have left me with only Rory, and even the other side agreed that would be a blood-bath. Terry had Jana firmly on his side again, and Hiram Heskell—smart, lawyerly, and still holding the voter-fraud incident against me because he wanted to be a judge someday. Marilee was ruled out from Terry's side because I successfully argued that she could be bought with a certain candy bar. Terry real-ized I was on to his Snickers-bribery scam and gave her up pretty quickly.

Mr. Samson had agreed to be our mediator. As he told me when I asked him, "Why not? It's not like I have anything else going on in my life."

We had gathered in Mr. Samson's classroom, turn-ing the desks to face one another while Mr. Samson sat at one end. "All right," he said, "I still don't know what this is about, but let's get started. What are we negotiating?"

"How to stay alive," I said. "Terry and I have been feuding since the first grade. It used to be all on his side but now I'm fighting back and it's starting to get . . . dangerous."

"I'll die if I have to," Terry said, crossing his arms.

"He's a novelist," Jana said to Mr. Samson. "He's full of dramatic feelings."

"Right," Mr. Samson said, glancing up to the sky like he wanted to make sure that God was viewing what his life had come to. "What are the terms?"

"I'll start," Jana said, waving her hand. "I have to protect Terry from his own feelings. Yes, he's willing to die, but I have to make sure that doesn't happen. I am literally Belinda Swankwell in *Vampires Have Feelings Too*."

Terry nodded in agreement. Apparently, he was totally on board with being Lance Stalwart to her Belinda Swankwell.

"Chadwick can't play any more tricks," Jana said. "Terry has too much important work to do on his novel."

"Wait a minute," I cried, "except for the last one, it's him always doing stuff to me!"

Suvi laid her hand on my arm and whispered, "I'll handle this." She turned to Jana and said, "I have counseled my client that an eye for an eye is the best course in this matter."

Terry reached up and covered one of his eyes like Suvi was sharpening a scalpel under the desk and preparing to take it from him on the spot.

"I will not stand by and allow my client to be victimized," Suvi continued, "just because your client is willing to die. Revenge, as they say, is a dish best served cold."

I had no idea what that was supposed to mean,

but I folded my arms and waited to see what they'd say to it.

Hiram removed his glasses and said to Suvi, "Let me clarify, your position is that if Terry remains firm in his willingness to die, then Chadwick will commit to dying also."

"Exactly," Suvi said.

"I'm not willing to die," I whispered to Suvi.

"It's just a negotiating tactic," Suvi muttered.

Rory stared at Terry. "This whole thing is stupid," he said. "Chadwick took your crayon, then you did all this stuff to get back at him, then he got back at you, then he gave you back your crayon. The. End. Go home and write your novel."

Terry leaned over and whispered something to Hiram. Hiram nodded and said, "My client would need assurances that he would not be subjected to any further pranks from your client or," he said, staring directly at Suvi, "be at any risk of losing an eye, before he agrees to go home and write his novel."

"My client," Suvi said, "would need assurances that Terry had ceased forever and forthwith any attempts at further pranks against *him*."

Mr. Samson softly groaned. "Let's wrap this up, shall we?"

"Unfortunately, Mr. Samson," Suvi said, "we cannot conclude this negotiation until we've determined how we enforce the terms. That is to say, how will we ensure that both parties comply with the agreement?"

Rory stood up. "I'll be Switzerland. If anything happens to either one of them, they can come to me and I'll get to the bottom of it. I know I'm Chadwick's friend and you'll think I'm biased, but I'm not. I've been telling him to give this up for years. It's even in my notebook, along with fake fingers, slingshots, walkie-talkies, Chex Mix, the school song, Jeeps, and Susie Townsend. I'm against them all."

"I would be amenable to that," Hiram said. "The parties could air any further disputes in a neutral Switzerland. I could make myself available to represent my client on an as-needed basis."

"Wait a minute," Terry said. "He can't be Switzerland and still be Chadwick's friend."

"Just because Rory is my friend doesn't mean he'll always be on my side," I said, desperate for a truce. "After all, he's not very reliable."

Rory shrugged, as if being unreliable was just part of his personality.

Suvi leaned forward and stared at Terry.

"All right!" Terry cried. "Just stop looking at my eyes!"

Suvi smiled. "So it's agreed that any further disputes will go directly to Rory's Switzerland. I've compiled the terms, now we just need all parties to sign it."

"Done!" Mr. Samson said. "Now I can go home to my crappy apartment and dwell on why I can't find anybody to marry me."

We all stood and moved to Mr. Samson's desk to sign the agreement. Peace was finally settling over the savannah.

Jana leaned over to Suvi and said, "What's going on? Is Chadwick your boyfriend?"

"Not yet," Suvi said.

I staggered but caught the edge of the desk before I fell to the ground. When had Suvi decided that? Could she just decide? Probably. Challenging one of Suvi's decisions would be like stealing an antelope out of a lion's jaws—not very likely. What did I think of it? It was hard to know. Whatever my true feelings were, they were buried somewhere under an avalanche of terror.

I took in a long, slow breath to steady my nerves. As I signed the truce between Terry and me, I started to think that pranks might end up being the least of my problems.

* * *

Terry and I went forward under the terms of an uneasy truce. It helped that I was now apparently part of a power couple. The synergy of Suvi had already improved my social standing. Whether that was because she was popular, or because everybody was afraid of her, I couldn't really tell. But the result was that I got some of my swagger back. Not like the summer's pool swagger; it was more of a medium-sized swagger. I decided it would be a mistake to get overconfident. After all, it was Suvi "going to the morgue and cutting out your eye" Singh who had brought Terry to the negotiating table, and not me. I would be like

Hank from *Mission Almost Impossible*—struggling but holding on anyway.

We finally found out what had really happened to Merriweather. Terry told Jana who told Marilee who reported it on the bleachers. Terry had been caught trying to smoke in the boys' bathroom. Merriweather had caught on not just from the smell of smoke but also from the coughing coming from a stall. Terry, seeing that he was cornered, lashed out like any crocodile would. He dunked his own head in the toilet and said he was going to tell everyone Merriweather did it. That had been the last straw for our emotionally fragile principal. He had peeled out of the parking lot in his Ford Fiesta one last time. According to Marilee, he was now in Pensacola, Florida, renting snorkel equipment to tourists. Staring at tropical fish helps him relax.